No more Unicorn Club . . .

"We need to have a club meeting," Jessica said. "If you guys can't make it, then—"

"Well, Jessica." Lila flipped her hair over her shoulder and glanced over toward Tommy. "You might find this hard to believe, but sometimes there are more important things in life than having a little meeting."

"So spending time with your boyfriends is more important than spending time with us?" Elizabeth asked. "Do you actually mean that?"

"You guys just don't understand," Mary said quietly.

"No, *you* don't understand," Jessica said. "Either you want to be our friends, and be Unicorns, or you don't. And if you don't come to that meeting tomorrow night, then I guess you don't want to be Unicorns anymore!"

"Well, if being a Unicorn means we have to spend every single second with you, then maybe you're right!" Mandy said.

"If our friendship isn't worth anything to you, then let's just forget about having a club," Elizabeth said.

The bell rang to start school, but I couldn't move. I couldn't believe it. Half the club had chosen having boyfriends over being Unicorns.

THE UNICORN CLUB™

UNICORNS IN LOVE

Written by
Alice Nicole Johansson

Created by
FRANCINE PASCAL

BANTAM BOOKS
NEW YORK · TORONTO · LONDON · SYDNEY · AUCKLAND

RL 4, 008-012

UNICORNS IN LOVE
A Bantam Book / May 1994

Sweet Valley High® and The Unicorn Club™
are trademarks of Francine Pascal

Conceived by Francine Pascal

Produced by Daniel Weiss Associates, Inc.
33 West 17th Street
New York, NY 10011

Cover art by James Mathewuse

ISBN: 0-553-48218-1
Published simultaneously in the United States and Canada

Bantam Books are published by Bantam Books, a division of Bantam
Doubleday Dell Publishing Group, Inc. Its trademark, consisting of the
words "Bantam Books" and the portrayal of a rooster, is Registered in U.S.
Patent and Trademark Office and in other countries. Marca Registrada.
Bantam Books, 1540 Broadway, New York, New York 10036.

PRINTED IN THE UNITED STATES OF AMERICA

OPM   0 9 8 7 6 5 4 3 2 1

To Alice Elizabeth Wenk

One

Hi. My name's Evie Kim. I'm five feet tall exactly—OK, maybe it's more like 4'11 and 3/4"—and I have long, thick, black hair. I'm Korean-American, and I live with my grandmother and her sister in a little house on the west side of Sweet Valley, California. My aunt and cousins live right down the street.

But why am I telling you all my vital statistics? I guess I feel kind of nervous, starting to tell such a big story. And I guess I have a tendency to talk a lot. I don't really mean to go on and on, it's just that— Oops, there I go again. I suppose the only thing to do is to just . . . well, start. I can't even believe everything that's been happening around here lately, and I've been dying to tell *somebody*.

The story really begins on the day that Mr. Drew posted the sign advertising auditions for the Sweet

Valley Middle School fall play. It was a play he'd written himself—he's done a lot of work as a screenwriter in Hollywood, and he's pretty good. He had a couple of big hit movies, one about a psycho baby-sitter and one about a haunted house with stairs that swallowed people up. But he got tired of the whole scene in Los Angeles, and so a couple of years ago he started teaching drama and theater arts at our school. But he still writes, and he'd come up with this whole, original play for us, which was really exciting.

The other exciting thing was that it wasn't just being done by the drama club—anyone at school who wanted to audition or be involved could try out. That meant it was going to be completely fun, watching new people on stage, people who normally didn't act in all the school plays.

"I'm definitely auditioning," Jessica Wakefield told me when we saw the poster in the hall after English class that day. We were on our way to lunch in the cafeteria. "And I *know* I'll get a part."

"Not too confident, are we?" Mandy Miller teased as she joined us. Both Jessica and Mandy are members of the Unicorn Club, and they've been friends for a long time. I only moved to Sweet Valley this summer, but already they had asked me to join the club, too, even though they are all seventh graders and I'm only in the sixth grade.

I felt really, incredibly lucky that they wanted me to join—the Unicorn Club is made up of some of the coolest girls at school, and I'm not just saying that because I'm in it. I mean it. All the members of the club have something special going for them. Like Jessica has this enthusiasm for everything, and she won't ever take no for an answer.

And Mandy's really funny, besides being the funkiest dresser this side of Los Angeles. She puts together cool outfits out of thrift-shop clothes, and she always looks terrific. She has long reddish-brown hair, and she's pretty in an unusual kind of way, like you might not notice it at first, but when you do, she seems gorgeous. Mandy's got this incredible will, too. She had cancer a year ago, and she's come through it amazingly well because she has this determination about her. You can tell she's not going to let anything get her down. She has tons of self-confidence, because of all the stuff she's been through. And she's involved in lots of extra-curricular things at school.

So I wasn't too surprised when she signed up on the list beside the poster asking for volunteers to help with sets, lighting, costumes, and all that other stuff. "Mandy Miller—Costume Designer," she wrote in her tiny handwriting.

"Put me down for that, too," I said. "But make it Assistant Costume Designer."

"No way." Mandy shook her head, then wrote, "Evie Kim—Co-costume Designer," and she put a "Co-" in front of her title, too. I smiled.

"It sounds like you have a stutter," Jessica said

as she borrowed Mandy's purple pen to write her name down on the list of people to audition. "Co-co-co-costume."

"That doesn't matter, since I'm not going to be the one onstage." Mandy grinned at Jessica. "But you are."

"Oh, I'm not worried. See, I don't get stage fright," Jessica said breezily as we walked into the cafeteria.

"Ever?" I asked. I've given tons of recitals—I play the violin—and I *still* get nervous every single time, even though nothing's ever gone wrong. I always think one of my strings is going to break or I'll drop my bow. I guess that's pretty stupid, seeing as how I've been playing for eight years now and everyone thinks I'm really good. I love playing the violin. I practice a couple of hours every day, and I take lessons from Mr. Santos, who's an incredible teacher. My grandmother's always saying that I'm "concert-career material," and she fantasizes about the day I make my big debut with an orchestra in Paris or Milan. I don't know about *that*, but I do love playing, and I plan to keep doing it as long as I can.

"Well, maybe when it's time for me to accept my first Academy Award I'll get nervous," Jessica said. "You know, with all those big stars around and being on TV and all."

"Love that modesty," Mandy said, shaking her head. "Hey, guys, what's up?" she called out to the other members of the Unicorn Club, who were already sitting at our special table in the cafeteria. It isn't ours, really—we just sit there every day, and nobody else ever does. We call it the Unicorner. Kind of corny, I know, but I like it anyway.

"Did you see the poster about the play?" Lila Fowler asked us as we sat down. She took a sip of cola and flipped her long brown hair over her shoulder. She always does that.

"Yeah, can you believe what it's called?" Jessica said. *"Tale of a Teenage Vampire."*

Maria Slater curled her lips, bared her teeth, and tried to look scary. The problem is, Maria's incredibly beautiful, with light brown skin and big brown eyes and the longest eyelashes ever. She couldn't quite pull off looking like a vampire.

I laughed. "I don't think you'll get the part of the vampire."

"You are going to try out, though, aren't you?" Elizabeth Wakefield, Jessica's identical twin, asked Maria. Elizabeth and Jessica look so much alike, I had a hard time figuring out who was who when I first met them. They both have shoulder-length blond hair and blue-green eyes, and they're exactly the same height and weight. Then I realized they always wear their hair differently: Jessica wears hers down around her shoulders, and Elizabeth puts hers into a ponytail or barrettes.

Also, they *act* completely differently. Jessica loves to lie on the couch with a bowl of popcorn and watch music videos for hours on end (not to mention sitcoms and cheesy romantic movies). She doesn't have a boyfriend right now, really, but she usually has her eye on someone, and she's been on a ton of dates, considering she's only thirteen. She's not the best student, although she is very smart—she's just not interested in classes. She comes to school for the social life more than anything—at least that's what Elizabeth says, to tease her.

Elizabeth takes school much more seriously than Jessica, but she's still a lot of fun to be around. She writes articles for the *7 & 8 Gazette* and also writes stories in her spare time. She plans to be a writer when she grows up, and I can just see her writing a best-selling mystery.

Maria nodded in response to Elizabeth's question. "Even if I only get a small part, I want to be involved." Maria used to be a child actress in Hollywood. I'd seen her in tons of television commercials and movies before I met her, through my grandmother, who also acted. I used to follow her around, hanging on her every word—I really sort of idolized her. But she and her family moved to Sweet Valley so she could take a break and just be a "normal" kid. Since I've met her again here, we're more like equals. I still think she's great, but I don't put her on a pedestal or anything. She did act in a movie called *Secondhand Rose* a while ago, but other than that she just goes to school and the mall like the rest of us now. "What about you, Evie?" Maria asked me. "Are you going to work on the play?"

"I'm going to do the costumes with Mandy," I said. Only the acting parts were decided by audition; anyone could volunteer for the other jobs.

Ellen Riteman opened a package of potato chips and crunched one loudly. "I want to get an acting role," she announced. "Something really good. Maybe one of the leads."

"You?" Lila asked. "Act?"

"Sure. Why not?" Ellen looked hurt.

"Oh, you just never have before, that's all," Lila said. "I'm kind of . . . surprised."

"So am I," Jessica said. "Do you have any idea how hard it is?"

Ellen ate another potato chip. "If you can do it, I can," she said.

Jessica looked at Lila and shrugged. The truth is, Ellen's really nice and sweet, but she does happen to be a bit of an airhead. No, make that a major airhead. I couldn't picture her remembering her lines any longer than five minutes, tops. But if she wanted to try, I wasn't going to stop her. Ellen's been a great friend to me—she was actually one of the first Unicorns to really warm up to me. Even though she's spacey, she'd never intentionally let you down, and she's great about doing nice things, like visiting people when they're sick and going out of her way to cheer people up when they're feeling kind of blue.

"I think I'll work on constructing the sets, or do the lighting or something," Elizabeth said. "I'm not sure I want to be in a vampire play."

"Chicken?" Mandy teased.

"No." Elizabeth grinned. "It's just that I have so much stuff to do, working for the *Gazette* and everything. I don't know if I have enough time to memorize lines."

"Building the sets takes a lot of time, too," Mary Wallace said. "But you know what? I think I'll do that with you, Elizabeth. It makes me too nervous to get on stage in front of everyone." Mary's nickname in the club is "Ms. Logical"—she's never done anything that didn't make one hundred percent sense. She has long, blond hair, and she's really cute.

"Yeah, with Mr. Drew being kind of half famous and having a well-known name and everything, I bet a *lot* of people are going to turn out," Lila said. "I mean, this has to be a really good production."

Jessica took a carrot stick out of her lunch bag. "So what are you going to do?"

"Be stage manager," Lila said. "Naturally."

Jessica groaned. She and Lila have been best friends for ages (I'm not sure exactly how long, because I just moved here and I didn't know them then and all). Anyway, half the time they seem totally irritated by each other. Lila's really rich—well, her dad is, anyway—and she tends to be bossy and thinks she's a little bit above everyone else. Except that lately she's been baby-sitting for a little girl named Ellie McMillan, who goes to the day-care center where we volunteer (I'll tell you more about that in a minute), and it seems to have made her nicer some-how. Like when Ellie ran away from home. Ellie got really upset because her mother started dating an old boyfriend. They spent so much time together, Mrs. McMillan didn't have much time for Ellie. So Ellie ran away to Lila's house, and Lila let her stay there for a while. Lila even got into heaps of trouble, be-cause she didn't want to betray Ellie. Now it's all straightened out, though, and Mrs. McMillan and her boyfriend, Mr. Stillman, are engaged!

"I wonder who they'll get to play the vampire," I said.

"It's going to be tough, since half the boys in this school qualify," Mandy joked, rolling her eyes.

"The vampire doesn't necessarily have to be a boy," Mary said.

"True." Mandy nodded. "Hey, Ellen, maybe that's the part for you. Let me see your fangs."

Ellen crumpled her napkin and threw it at Mandy.

"But seriously, if the vampire *is* a boy . . . and vampires always come to suck the blood of their victims . . . what if one of us has to kiss him?" Jessica asked.

"Then it *really* matters who gets that part," Maria said, nodding.

"Oh, come on, it won't be that bad," Elizabeth said. "Anyway, it's just acting, right? You're only pretending to kiss."

"There's no such thing," Jessica said. "I mean, if you kiss somebody, you kiss them—period."

"Personally, I can't wait," Ellen said. "I think this is going to be the best play ever done here. I mean, Mr. Drew used to work in Hollywood. This might be the premiere of something they turn into a big play, or a movie, or—"

"Don't get too excited," Mary said. "We haven't even seen the script yet."

"Oh, it'll be good," Lila said. "I trust Mr. Drew."

If we had known what was going to happen when we started that play, we might all wish we'd never seen that poster, and that Mr. Drew had never written a play about a teenage vampire.

But we didn't know, so we had to find out the hard way. My grandmother says that's the best way to learn something, but I don't know. I think I could have done without a lot of the stuff the Unicorn Club went through all because of Mr. Drew's *Tale of a Teenage Vampire*.

But I'm getting too far ahead of myself. Let me back up and tell you the whole story, from beginning to end.

Two

After school, Mandy and I went over to the Attic, the vintage clothing store my grandmother owns. I help her out whenever I have time, and Mandy just likes hanging out at the store because she's so into old clothes, and she likes helping Grandma set up the window displays.

Actually, my grandmother's store has more than clothing—she also sells antique furniture like love seats and dining tables, and cool old lamps and appliances like blenders and toasters from the 1950s. When she started the store, she was selling a lot of her own stuff. You see, when we moved here from Los Angeles, she had a huge house full of stuff, and we moved in with my great-aunt. Her place is much smaller than Grandma's old place. (My grandmother's been taking care of me ever since my parents died, when I was six.) She has incredible taste, and everyone loved her furniture so much they bought it right away. So since she sold a lot of those things, she's been shopping at auctions and estate sales. She brings the things she buys in to sell at her store.

My grandmother used to be a pretty major actress. She's been in a lot of movies—she even filmed a diaper commercial with Maria once, way back when Maria was a baby, if you can believe that—and she's still a great actress. Only since she's about fifty-five now, she hasn't been getting any parts. She's really beautiful, with long, straight black hair sprinkled with gray. I know she sometimes gets sad about not acting anymore, but most of the time she seems really happy. I keep telling her she should join the local acting club, but she just laughs and shakes her head. I couldn't wait to tell her that I was going to work on the play.

"Hi, Grandma," I said when we walked into the store. She was standing behind the antique wood sales desk, working on something.

She waved her hand in the air. "Hold on a second, I'm adding." She scribbled something, then looked up. "Hello, you two. How was school?"

"Not too bad. I mean, we lived through lunch," Mandy joked.

"Grandma, we have some really exciting news," I said. "We're going to be working on a play at school—a new play, one Mr. Drew wrote." I dropped my backpack full of books onto the floor behind the sales desk and set my violin case carefully on top of it.

"No kidding," Grandma said. "But you didn't mention anything about auditioning. When did all this happen?"

"Oh, it hasn't, yet," Mandy explained. "They only announced it today. Evie and I signed up to take care of the costumes. Hey, do you think you could be our costume consultant?"

"Yeah, you are an expert," I said.

My grandmother shrugged. "Sure, I'll help, if I have time. You know you can borrow anything from the store you want to. Hey, don't you have a big semiformal coming up at school next month?" she asked. "You two ought to pick your dresses for that before you give anything away to the play."

"Grandma," I said, rolling my eyes.

"What's that look for?" she asked.

"I probably won't even go," I said.

"Of course you will," Mandy said.

"It's not like I'm going to have a date or anything," I said.

Mandy hit me on the arm with a black feather boa. "Evie, don't say that. I bet there're lots of guys who'd want to go with you. And anyway, you don't *have* to have a date."

"Mandy's right," my grandmother said. "And there's no reason you couldn't invite a boy to go with you, either."

I shook my head, and my long hair fanned out

around my face. "No way. Never." I'm not shy in general, but when it comes to talking to boys, I don't know. I kind of turn into a mouse, especially when I really like someone. I hate when that happens. My grandmother says I'll get better at it as I get older. I just hope she's right.

"Well, we'll just see about that," Mandy said. "OK, Clara, this play's about a vampire. What do you have for today's hip vampire to wear?"

My grandmother went into the back room, where she keeps the really odd stuff. She came out carrying a shiny black cape, with purple moons embroidered into the fabric and silver sparkles. "How about this?"

"Maybe Mr. Drew should call this the Halloween play," Mandy joked, and I laughed.

The auditions were held on a Wednesday, and on Friday, all the people who had won roles had their names printed in a special box in the *7 & 8 Gazette*, one of the school papers (the other was *The Sixers*, which was put out by sixth graders). I wasn't too surprised to see Maria's name on the list, or Jessica's, either—but Ellen had actually gotten one of the big roles, as one of the girlfriends of the vampire! I wondered if Mr. Drew knew what he was getting himself into. But then I decided I shouldn't sell Ellen short. I mean, maybe she *could* be a good actress. At least she was trying, and she does have a flair for acting dramatic.

Then I skimmed the list to see who the vampire was: Rick Hunter. Rick was a really cute eighth grader. And he was nice, too. I mean, I didn't know him very well, because I was still so new at school, but he seemed pretty nice to me. And I have to say that if there were going to be any kissing scenes, it wouldn't be half bad. . . . But of course, I was going to be working on costumes. I didn't have to worry about that.

We started rehearsals for the play that afternoon, after a brief meeting. A lot of people were going to be working on it—it seemed as though everyone was excited about being in an all-school play. There must have been about forty of us at that first meeting. Mr. Drew said he wanted the play to be ready in a month, which seemed way too soon, but I guess he was used to working with tight deadlines and everything. Soon everyone broke up into groups—actors, set designers, lighting people, and costume designers (me and Mandy). We holed up in a corner of the auditorium to read the script. Mandy and I needed to figure out what kinds of outfits people would be wearing so we could start either sewing or looking for them right away.

The plot of the play went kind of like this: A fourteen-year-old boy moves with his family to a new school in Florida. But on the way, they stop at a big amusement park, and the boy—his name is Victor—goes on a ride called the Blood Line. It's a train ride through all these creepy scenes, and

Dracula's in it and everything. (Dracula even comes out and sort of snaps his jaws at the people on the ride as they pass by in one of those little trains.) Well, something really weird happens on that ride, because Victor gets touched by the Dracula guy (even though it's only someone in costume), and afterward, every Saturday, he turns into a vampire.

Only instead of wanting to suck his victims' blood, he starts drinking tons of soda pop. Then he does strange things, like trying to climb up the goalposts on the football field, or dancing wildly at the school party. For some reason he becomes incredibly cute to girls, and any girl he kisses ends up with the same problem. Pretty soon the whole school is acting really weird, and the principal, the teachers, and the parents are all trying to figure out why. It ends with the home economics and nutrition teacher brewing up an antivampire potion, and Victor falling in love with his first victim, Mallory Maraschino. (I'm not kidding, that's really her name. Mr. Drew has a bizarre view of things.)

Sound complicated? It is. I wondered if Mr. Drew was going to be able to pull it off, there were so many special effects.

"This kind of reminds me of *The Slime That Ate Sweet Valley*," Mandy said when she was finished reading. She tossed the script onto the floor. "That's a movie we made here last year. It was pretty gross, but really funny, too."

"I think the costumes will be easy," I said.

"There's not much in here except a bunch of kids at high school."

"True." Mandy nodded. "But we want them to look interesting. And I think whenever someone's going to start acting weird, they should have some kind of sign to tell the audience that—like a weird hat or something."

"That's a good idea," I said. "And we can make Victor dress really weird or eccentric."

"Yeah, it says in here that he just moved from New York City. Maybe he brought a bunch of funky clothes with him, and he *totally* doesn't fit in, which makes everyone think he's even stranger at first." Mandy laughed. "OK, maybe that's my life, not his."

I laughed, too. "No, I think that sounds good. It'll be fun putting Rick in outrageous outfits. All he ever wears are rugby shirts and jeans."

"Hey, how's it going, you guys?" Mary asked as she and Elizabeth walked over to us. They were both going to work on designing and building the sets with Peter DeHaven, Tommy Rivera, and the woodworking teacher, Mr. Yates. "Did you read the script yet?"

I nodded. "Pretty funny stuff."

"I think it'll be great," Elizabeth said. "I don't know how we'll get it all ready in four weeks, though."

"I guess we'll have to work a lot of evenings," Mandy said.

"No kidding—like every night," I said. "Can

you imagine having to learn all those lines in just a few weeks?"

"We're going to be really busy," Mary agreed. "But I think it'll be fun. Especially with so many people working on it." Mary looked around the auditorium, and I glanced up at the stage, where Rick and Ellen were reading through their first scene in the script out loud.

"Like who?" Mandy prompted.

"What do you mean?" Mary asked.

Mandy grinned. "I've seen you look at Rick about eight million times today."

Mary's face turned pink. "Well . . . I guess I do have kind of a crush on him."

"I knew it," Mandy said. "That's cool. He's nice, and he has a great sense of humor. I think you guys would have a lot of fun together if you went on a date. Seems like you like a lot of the same things."

"Sure, if he liked *me*," Mary said. "Which he doesn't. Anyway, you sound like a computer dating service."

"You don't *know* that he doesn't like you," Elizabeth said. "Why wouldn't he? Anyway, since we'll be spending so much time here, maybe you can get to know him better."

"Next thing you know, you'll be dancing arm in arm at the fall semiformal." Mandy took my hand and pulled me to my feet, then started waltzing up the aisle of the auditorium, humming the Wedding March.

"Cut it out!" I giggled. I could tell everyone was looking at us—some people were laughing.

"Excuse me, girls, but we're trying to produce a play here," Mr. Drew said from the stage. "Would you mind practicing your dancing another time?"

"No problem," Mandy said. "I think we're learning the polka in gym class next week—I'll wait for that."

I just shook my head. Being around Mandy is always a lot of fun, but she does get us into trouble sometimes.

That Saturday Ellen, Jessica, and I took some of the kids from the day-care center to the Sweet Valley Science Museum. It's not a huge museum, but it's fun—there are lots of activities, especially for little kids. We'd already been to the computer section, where there are lots of interactive games, and to a special kind of movie that's shown on a huge screen. It feels like you're right in the middle of whatever's happening onscreen. The kids really loved that.

Let me explain about the kids. The Unicorn Club started volunteering at the day-care center a little while ago when they got into trouble at school with our principal, Mr. Clark. He "sentenced" the girls in the club to thirty hours there, each, because Lila and Jessica were having this silly dare war that caused all kinds of problems. Anyway, after working there for a while, all the Unicorns decided they really liked it. Now at least two of us volunteer there three times a week, and on some afternoons we're almost all there. Then on some Saturdays we try to plan something for the kids to do outside the center, something they might not get a chance to do with their parents.

The day-care center is operated by the Sweet Valley Community Services Organization, which runs a lot of projects for families who need some help. They offer counseling, shelters for homeless people, and other support services, including day care, which gives parents the time to work, or to look for work. Mrs. Willard is the director of the center, and she's nice, although she's very strict about our taking our responsibility to the kids seriously.

That makes sense, though. We've gotten really close to some of the kids, and it would be wrong of us to ignore them just because we were busy. They depend on us. And that's cool, because we're really fond of them, too. They take my mind off whether I got an A on my algebra test, or which piece I'll be playing at my next recital, or whether I should wear my red sweater or my blue one to school the next day.

I especially like hanging out there because I don't have any younger brothers or sisters. It means I get to have the kids for a couple of hours at a time, then I can go home to my own room and have all the privacy I want.

At the moment, all the kids were in the middle

of a huge dinosaur—a balloon dinosaur, that is. It was one of those things with clear sides and a big, springy floor. Kids can jump up and down in there for hours and fly all around and not get hurt. I don't know what it has to do with science, but I guess it gets out all the kids' energy. Then they don't run around wrecking skeleton displays or trying to ride the giant stuffed elks. I think they call it the antigravity machine.

I watched Yuky, a little Korean-American girl, jumping up and down and shrieking in the middle of the dinosaur. "I wouldn't want to be the museum monitor in there," I said to Jessica, who was standing next to me.

"Me either." She grimaced as Oliver Washington screamed at the top of his lungs before flying across the dinosaur's "belly." "That kid is so loud."

I smiled. Jessica's always half-complaining about Oliver, but we all know she really loves him. Whenever she walks into the Center, he yells her name and tries to tackle her. She's almost like a big sister to him. That's kind of how I feel about Yuky, I guess because we're both Korean-American. Everyone says we look like sisters. I like Yuky because she has so much energy, even if sometimes it's a little out of control. And I like her parents, too—I've met them a couple of times. They keep saying they'll have me over for dinner soon. I can't wait. It'll be nice to get to know them better.

Oliver, Yuky, and Arthur came running out of the

dinosaur bubble. "That was fun!" Yuky exclaimed.

"Now what?" Oliver asked, panting after jumping around so much.

"Well, how about if we go on over to the thing
we saw when we came in—you know, the physics
exhibit?" I asked them.

Arthur frowned. "What's that?"

"It's the thing in the big glass case, where a little
metal ball drops down, and it sets off all these
other things," Ellen told him. "Remember? You
wanted to see that?"

"Oh, yeah! Let's go!" Arthur cried.

We each took one kid's hand and moved
through the crowd, down the hallway to the physics room, right near the entrance. There was a
crowd around the big glass case, but we managed
to squeeze in so the kids could see.

"So how's your part in the play?" I asked Jessica
as the kids watched the ball drop and start to run
through the entire contraption. It set off a chain re-
action of tipping levers and flapping gates. "I
didn't get a chance to talk to you about it yet."

"Not bad," Jessica said. "Actually, I have kind of
a strange role. You read the script, right?" I nodded. "Did you see that character called the
Freshman?"

"The Freshman . . . Doesn't she go around making comments on everything that's happening?" I
asked, just as the kids squealed because the ball
dropped and made a bell go off.

"Right," Jessica said. "She's like the— What do you call it when someone kind of interprets things for the audience?"

"The narrator?" I asked.

Jessica nodded. "That's it. So I get to be in almost every scene, but it's like I'm just commenting on what's happening, and then I run offstage. My lines are pretty funny, though."

"I'm so glad we both get to be in the play," Ellen said, coming up behind Jessica.

"Yeah, that is pretty cool," I said. "I can't wait to see you guys do some scenes together."

"What's even neater is that I get to do a bunch of scenes with Tim Davis." Ellen sighed and leaned against me. "He is just so adorable. Did you see that sweatshirt he was wearing today, with the ripped cuffs and the big letters on it?"

"He *was* kind of a jerk to Mary last year," Jessica reminded her. "Remember when he asked her out to that picnic, and then her bike broke down and he didn't even wait up for her—she had to walk by herself?"

"Yeah, that's true, but Mary didn't even really want to go out with him. Janet was the one who fixed them up," Ellen said. "It's not like she was hurt."

"OK, maybe so, but have you ever noticed that all he ever wants to talk about is basketball and how great he is?" I commented. "He does have kind of a big head."

"Yeah, but that's because he really is good. Anyway, I don't think he'll act like a jerk. I think he's changed." Ellen smiled dreamily. "He's acting totally nice to me. Get this—he already asked me if I wanted to skip lunch with him sometime next week so we could do some extra rehearsing."

"What about Rick? You actually get to kiss him," Jessica teased. She leaned forward and gave Oliver's arm a squeeze. "Having fun?"

He nodded eagerly. "This thing is so cool. I want to watch it again!"

"Rick's OK," Ellen told Jessica. "But that kiss is just acting. Tim . . ." Ellen sighed again.

Is everyone around here suddenly talking about boys a lot, or what? I wondered. It seemed as though ever since the play had been announced, everyone was falling for someone new. I wondered if I was supposed to have a crush on someone, too. But I didn't, at least not right that second.

Maybe Mr. Drew should have called his play *Tale of a Teenager in Love*, I thought. No, make that teenagers, plural. It seemed that everyone was falling in love—everyone except me.

Three

We started working on the play every afternoon, and some evenings, too, because students who played on sports teams couldn't make the afternoon rehearsals. The actors broke into groups and worked on their scenes individually. I didn't really know what was up, except for the updates from everyone at lunch.

It was Thursday, during the first week of rehearsals, when things started to get weird. Not as weird as in Mr. Drew's play, but still pretty strange. Good strange, I guess.

Mandy and I were supposed to be having a meeting with the set designers to make sure we were headed in the same direction. We didn't want the clothes to clash with the sets or vice versa. So Mandy, Elizabeth, Mary, Peter DeHaven, and Tommy Rivera, an eighth grader, and I all got together in the art studio. Lila, the stage manager, was there, too.

"OK, people. What do you have so far?" Lila asked the group after we had all arrived.

I got out our sketches and some sample clothes Mandy and I had found at the Attic. I started to show Lila what each one was for. "This is Carmen's dress for the dance scene," I said, pointing to a sketch of an old-fashioned green and yellow dress with a ruffled skirt.

"I know it looks geeky, but she does play a geek," Mandy said.

Elizabeth and I laughed. "And this is for Rick's first scene, when he goes to the amusement park." I showed everyone the plain white polo shirt and very faded blue denim shorts. "Kind of plain, but his clothes get more interesting later on. We didn't want him to clash with the vampire in the ride, and plus, he has to show up in the dark."

After a few more outfits, I noticed Lila wasn't even listening or paying attention to me. She was just sitting there, staring into Tommy's dark eyes, and he was looking right back at her!

"Ahem." I cleared my throat as loudly as I could, while still trying to be polite. "Ahem!"

Lila turned back toward me, a dreamy look on her face. "Oh, I'm sorry, Evie. What were you saying?"

"Well, this is what we thought Jessica should wear, but Mandy was wondering if maybe it should be something sort of nerdy, since she is just called 'the Freshman,'" I explained. "Mandy, do you have those plans for Jessica's clothes?" I looked to my left, where Mandy had been sitting—only now she was leaning over Peter's shoulder. He was pointing out some of his set ideas to her.

"Oh, that looks terrific," she said to him. "Wow, you really have a talent for this stuff."

He shrugged and looked a little shy, which is easy for Peter to do. He hardly ever says a word. "I'm OK at it. I'm not half as good as you are at clothes, though."

Mandy smiled. "Thanks, that's really nice."

What is this, the Mutual Admiration Society? I wanted to ask. I looked at Elizabeth, and she just looked back at me and shrugged. "So, Elizabeth and Mary, you want to go over the plans together?" I asked them.

"We might as well," Elizabeth said. "I doubt any of the others would mind."

Peter and Mandy were wrapped up in a conversation, and Lila was sitting down at the desk next to Tommy.

"What's going on around here? It's like Valentine's Day or something," Mary said.

"I know," Elizabeth said. "I've never seen Lila or Mandy act so goofy before. They must really like those guys."

"Well, that's great," I said. "No, I mean it—I'm really happy for them. I just hope all this lovey-dovey stuff doesn't ruin the play."

"Oh, it won't," Mary said confidently. "I'm sure it's just because everyone isn't used to spending so much time together." She leaned closer. "I had no idea Lila liked Tommy."

"Me either," I said. I looked at the two of them. Tommy is tall, with shortish brown hair, and he always dresses in pretty trendy (but nice) clothes. He's totally cute, but he didn't seem like Lila's type for some reason. From what I'd heard from everyone else, I thought she usually liked guys that were older, more sophisticated. Tommy was just an average, nice guy. "It looks like they get along pretty well, though."

Elizabeth nodded. "Tommy *is* really nice," she whispered, just as Lila cracked up laughing at something he had said. Lila looked so happy—I couldn't remember ever seeing her smile so much. Maybe she really *was* in love.

"You're not going to believe it!" Mary cried, running after me and Elizabeth when we left rehearsal the next afternoon. She had been filling in, rehearsing a scene with Rick, because Carmen Manning was home sick with the flu. Mr. Drew didn't want to waste any rehearsal time, especially when Rick had so many lines to remember.

"We're not going to believe what?" Elizabeth asked.

"I stood in for Carmen's part, right?" Mary asked, all out of breath when she caught up to us halfway across the school parking lot.

"Right," I said. "How did it go? You just read the script, didn't you?"

Mary nodded as we all started walking down the sidewalk together. I had to get home to have a quick dinner before my violin lesson with Mr. Santos at six o'clock. He was so nice, he had completely rescheduled my lessons so I could work on the play. "I don't know why you're not in the orchestra instead," he said to me when I told him about working on costumes. I had to explain that Sweet Valley Middle School didn't exactly rate an orchestra for our plays. More like a good stereo system, if we were lucky.

"Rick kept smiling at me the whole time we were in this funny kind of love scene," Mary said. "It was so cool."

"No offense, but wasn't he supposed to smile?" Elizabeth asked. "I mean, wasn't it scripted?"

Mary shook her head. "No. If anything, he was supposed to be confused. And he told me afterward he was really glad Mr. Drew asked me to play the role, even if it was just for one day. He said he likes working with me a lot more than with Carmen. And *then* he said, 'So do you want to see that new movie over at the Quad?' " Mary practically yelled. Then she turned around, to make sure no one was following us.

"You're kidding," Elizabeth said. "So was he asking you to go with him?"

Mary nodded eagerly. "Yes! We're going tomorrow night. He actually asked me to go to a movie with him. I felt like I was going to faint."

"But you didn't, did you?" Elizabeth asked. "I mean, you did stay conscious long enough to say yes, didn't you?"

Mary nodded, grinning. "Yeah. He said he'd meet me there at seven, and then maybe we could grab something to eat afterward."

"So it's a real date!" I said excitedly. "That's great, Mary. Wow, I can't believe it."

"You mean you can't believe he likes me? I can't, either," Mary said. "I mean, a couple of days ago I didn't even think he knew who I *was*, and now—"

"No, not that, stupid." I swatted her on the arm. "Of course he should like you, because you're great. What I meant was, I can't believe all of a sudden everyone has a boyfriend. First Lila, then Mandy, now you."

"Rick's not my boyfriend yet," Mary said. "I mean, what if we have a rotten time tomorrow night? What if I act totally stupid?"

Elizabeth shook her head. "That won't happen."

"You know what? There's something really weird going on," I said. "Weird in a good kind of way." I grinned at Mary, who was so happy she was almost skipping down the sidewalk.

"I wonder who's next," Elizabeth said.

"You make it sound like we're coming down with a fever," Mary said.

"Well, it is kind of like that," Elizabeth said, laughing.

"Then you'd better look out—it's highly contagious," Mary teased, grabbing Elizabeth's arm.

The next day, Friday, I got to lunch before everyone else. I picked up a tray, got a salad and some soup, and sat down at the table in the Unicorner.

I saw Ellen come in with Tim, and waved to her. She waved back and smiled, but instead of coming over to sit with me, she followed Tim to a table clear across the cafeteria. A minute later, Mandy walked in. She looked over at me and waved, then took her lunch and went over to sit with Peter DeHaven at a table with his friends. For a few minutes, I thought I was going to be eating lunch all by myself, but then Jessica came in and sat down with me.

"Where is everyone?" she asked, taking a sandwich out of her purple nylon lunch bag.

"Ellen's over there," I said, pointing to Tim and his tall friends from the basketball team. "And Mandy's sitting with Peter."

Jessica looked a little surprised, but just then Elizabeth and Maria came in and sat down at our table, so she didn't say anything. We all started talking about our plans for the weekend, which included a trip to the mall, since this was the first Saturday in a while that we weren't doing something with the kids from the Center.

"It feels kind of funny, not spending so much time over there because of all the rehearsals," Maria said. "Doesn't it?"

Jessica nodded. "I miss Oliver."

"We're lucky Mrs. Willard had some new volunteers to cover our shifts," Elizabeth said. "But next week, I should be able to spend more time there. The sets are coming along great. I think I only have to help paint twice a week or so."

"I can go to the Center with you," I said. "Mandy and I don't have to work on the costumes too much anymore—we've gotten everything figured out, almost, and some stuff is being sewn. We can't do any fittings or anything until it's done."

"Hey, Mary!" Jessica called.

"Hi, you guys!" Mary replied as she walked past us. Rick was right behind her, and the two of them went straight into the lunch line together to get their lunches.

Lila came into the cafeteria a second later. She walked right over to the Unicorner.

"Finally, *someone* who has a boyfriend is going to sit with us," I heard Jessica mutter under her breath.

"Hey, guys, what's up?" Lila asked, smiling.

"Not much," Elizabeth said. "We were just talking about the kids at the Center."

"I haven't been there all week," Lila said. "I feel terrible. I told Ellie I'd see her this week, and I haven't even been there once."

"Well, maybe we can all find an afternoon next week when we can go," Maria said. "Hey, didn't

Mr. Drew say something about not having rehearsals on Tuesday?"

"Yeah, he has to go to a meeting," I said. "We all get the afternoon off."

"Then let's all definitely go then," Jessica said. "So are you going to sit down or what?" she asked Lila.

"Oh, well, I promised Tommy I'd eat with him," Lila said. "Sorry. Have you seen him?"

"I think he's over there with Tim and Ellen," I said.

"Great! See you later!" Lila called over her shoulder as she made her way past the table in front of ours. I watched as Tommy stood up and waved to Lila, a big grin on his face.

"He is totally crazy about her," Maria said. "Look at how happy he is to see her!"

"Lila's lucky—Tommy seems sweet," Elizabeth added. "I bet they'll go out for a long time."

Jessica pulled in the chair next to her. "So what time are we meeting at the mall tomorrow?"

"One o'clock," Maria said. "By the fountain, as usual."

"I can't wait to do some decent shopping," Jessica said. "I feel like all I've been doing lately is memorizing lines."

"That's because that's all you *have* been doing," Elizabeth said. "You guys should see Jessica—every night she stands in front of the mirror in the bathroom and tries to recite her lines."

"Admit it—I'm getting pretty good at them," Jessica said.

Elizabeth nodded. "I kind of hate to ask this, be-cause I don't want to seem mean, but how's Ellen doing with hers?"

Maria shrugged. "We haven't been rehearsing the same scenes, so I don't know. But she must be doing pretty well, or else Mr. Drew would replace her."

"Well, you guys are going to get a kick out of this," I told them. "She told me she read all her lines into a tape recorder, and she's playing it back to herself while she sleeps."

"No way!" Maria cracked up laughing.

"She read about it in some magazine, how you can learn while you sleep," I said.

Elizabeth shrugged. "If it works for her, then I guess it doesn't matter how lame it sounds."

"I just hope she doesn't mess up and forget her lines, because we'll all look bad," Jessica said.

"She won't," Maria said. "I mean, she might be spacey sometimes, but not when it really counts. Anyway, we still have almost three weeks to get ready."

Jessica didn't look convinced.

"So tell me all about your date," I said to Mary that night. "I want to know everything. Did you have fun?" Mary had called to tell me about her movie date with Rick.

I was lying on my bed, curling the phone cord around my finger. I don't have my own phone, though—I just pull the one in the upstairs hall into my room when I want to talk privately (which is most of the time). My room's not too big, but it's plenty big enough for me. I have my bed over by the windows, and on the other side of the room is my collection of music stuff: my tape player, my violin and all my sheet music and the music stand, and even some posters of composers—and one of Johnny Buck, which totally doesn't fit in, but I like it. Mary used to have the hugest crush on him, and she's seen him in concert about five times. Jessica has, too.

"Well, we met at the Quad at seven to see that movie about the guy who goes to Russia on special assignment," Mary said. "It wasn't bad, but you know what? I don't even think I heard half of it, because I was so nervous. At a scary part Rick actually held my hand, can you believe it?"

"What a sweetheart."

"Yeah. Then we went over to that pizza place near the mall and got a slice and a soda," Mary said. "He was even going to pay for mine, but I wouldn't let him."

"That's so nice," I said. "Rick sounds like the perfect date."

"That's not even the best part," Mary said. "Evie, he asked me to go to the semiformal!"

"You're kidding!" I said.

"Nope. He said he'd wanted to ask me before, but since he didn't know me that well, he felt like he couldn't," Mary said. She sighed. "I still can't get over it—Rick Hunter and me, going to the big fall semiformal."

"Wow," I said. "You guys must have really hit it off."

"Definitely. I mean, it's like we have tons to talk about. We never run out of things to say." Mary paused for a minute. "I know I've only been on one date and everything, but I really like him. It sounds crazy," Mary went on. "I'll probably jinx the whole thing. But I just can't stop thinking about him."

"Don't worry, you won't jinx it," I told her. "He really likes you, too—he asked you to the dance, right?"

After I finished talking to Mary, I put on the silk pajamas my grandmother had bought for me on a trip to Hong Kong for a movie a few years ago (she'd bought them extra huge, and I was only now growing into them). Then I lay in bed, listening to one of my favorite Bach violin concertos on cassette, and stared at the ceiling. I wondered if I would be lucky enough to fall in love someday. I tried to imagine who the perfect boy for me would be. But since I hadn't met him yet, it was hard.

Mary's so lucky, I thought, just before I drifted off to sleep.

Four

"How was your lesson?" my grandmother asked when I came in the door on Saturday around noon. I had to drop off my violin and get some money before going to the mall to meet everyone.

"Fine," I said. "Mr. Santos said he's planning another recital for me and his other students in about two months."

"Two months. But that's forever to wait to hear you play." My grandmother smiled.

"Grandma, you only hear me every single day when I practice," I said. "Besides, two months is barely enough time for me to get ready. He wants me to perform a piece that's about twenty minutes long!"

"No problem," Grandma said with a wave of her hand.

"Sure, no problem for *you*," I teased. "You just have to sit there and listen." I glanced at the clock above the refrigerator. "Oops. I'd better go or I'll be late."

She got her purse off the kitchen table, took out her wallet, and handed me a ten-dollar bill. "This is for earrings or makeup or whatever."

"I don't need this much, Grandma," I said. "Just enough for an ice cream or something is fine." Since my grandmother had stopped getting so many acting roles, we hadn't had very much money. But she'd done a local commercial a few weeks ago, and with the store's business picking up, I guess we were doing OK—better than when we first moved to Sweet Valley, at least.

"No, that's OK. We can afford it. Just don't spend too much, and if you see something you like for the dance, have them hold it. We can go back later and I'll take a look at it," my grandmother told me before I went out the door. Even though it was Saturday, one of the Attic's busiest days, she was taking the morning off to do some work around the house. My aunt and great-aunt would mind the store. "OK?"

"OK," I said, then I kissed her cheek.

As I rode my bicycle to the mall to meet everyone, I thought about what it would be like if my mother were still around. Since she died when I was so young, I never really got used to doing things with her. But sometimes I wondered whether we'd do stuff like go to the mall together.

Or maybe to the movies, or on trips. Don't get me wrong, I love my grandmother very much, and it's much easier living with her than you might think—we get along incredibly well and hardly ever argue. But every once in a while I wish my mom were around, too.

I locked my bike in the rack by the mall's south entrance, which is closest to the fountain where we always meet. I was a couple of minutes late, so when I hurried in I expected to find everyone standing there, waiting for me. Instead, only Jessica, Elizabeth, and Maria were there.

"Hi, Evie. How are you doing?" Elizabeth greeted me.

I slumped onto the bench beside Jessica. "I'm exhausted."

"How can you be tired? It's Saturday," Maria said.

"I slept until eleven," Jessica said. "And I feel great."

"I had a lesson this morning," I explained. "And on Saturdays, Mr. Santos always keeps me an extra half hour because he doesn't have anyone coming in after me."

"I can't wait until you start playing with orchestras in New York, and the newspapers say how great you are," Elizabeth said.

I laughed. "Yeah, OK. So where's everyone else?" I leaned over and looked at Jessica's watch. It was ten after one.

"I don't know, but I'm ready to shop," Jessica

said. "If they don't show up in the next five minutes, I think we should start without them."

"It's not that late yet. I hope they remember.
When I talked to Mary last night, I forgot to remind
her," I said. "She said she had a great time at the
movies with Rick."

"That's good," Maria said. "Didn't Ellen go out
with Tim, too?"

Elizabeth nodded. "I think they went bowling."
A few minutes later, she looked at her watch, then
got up and walked in a circle around the fountain.
"I didn't see anybody," she announced.

"I cannot believe the nerve of some people,"
Jessica said, vigorously tapping her foot against the
floor. "We've been waiting here twenty minutes already! I have better things to do with my Saturday
than sit around and—"

"Calm down," Elizabeth interrupted her. "So
they're a little late—OK, a lot. It's not like you're
never late, Jessica."

"True, but I'm only late to unimportant things,
like school," Jessica replied.

"Uh-huh." Elizabeth nodded. "Sure you are."

"Anyway, that's *four* people who aren't here,"
Jessica went on.

"Look, it's almost one thirty," Maria said. "They
must not be coming. We might as well get going."

"I agree." Jessica stood up. "It's their loss if we
end up with better dresses than they do for the
semiformal."

"Don't think of it that way," Elizabeth urged. "I'm sure they just forgot, or their parents had something else for them to do."

Jessica frowned. "Well, whatever. Let's just get to Verve before all the great dresses are gone!"

I looked at Elizabeth and shrugged. Jessica does tend to react a little dramatically, but this was a little much, even for her. Still, I couldn't remember the last time half the Unicorn Club didn't show up to meet the other half.

"I'm sure there's some explanation," I said to Elizabeth. "I hope nothing's wrong, like no one got in a car accident or anything."

"Don't worry," Elizabeth said. "We'll talk to them later. So what kind of dress are you looking for?"

About two hours later, after we'd gone in and out of every single clothing store the Valley Mall had to offer, and tried on about a zillion dresses, skirts, and sweaters, I was completely discouraged—and exhausted. Nothing makes me more tired than trying on a bunch of clothes that look stupid on me. I feel like when you're twelve, everything's for someone either four years older or four years younger. I saw some nice dresses that would have looked great on me if I were sixteen (kind of slinky, with sequins) or cute on me if I were eight (lots of ruffles). But nothing in between.

"We're not going to give up," Elizabeth said to

me. "I bet if we come back in a week or so, they'll
have new stuff."

"Hey, I don't know about you guys, but I could
really go for something to eat," Maria said.

"Me, too," Jessica said. She shifted her shopping
bag to her other hand. She'd bought a gorgeous
oversized V-neck sweater with a floral pattern on
it. "What do you feel like having?"

"Not pizza," Elizabeth said. "We had that last
night."

"Let's go to Casey's," Maria suggested. "I'd love
some frozen yogurt."

"Good idea," I said. "I'm so hungry, I think I'll
have a Banana Super Split."

"You?" Jessica grinned. "The queen of the single
scoop?"

I smiled. "I know I don't usually eat that much,
but I'm starving. I didn't have lunch today."
Sometimes when I get busy, I forget to eat. My
grandmother's always telling me I have to eat
more, but when I get caught up in whatever I'm
doing, it just doesn't seem important—until I wind
up out of energy and so hungry I could eat my violin bow.

We walked down to Casey's, our favorite ice
cream place. It has some booths, and also some
small tables, and on any given day there are about
a dozen kids from school there. They have a cool
jukebox, and you can sit there for an hour without
anyone rushing you to give up your table. We went

in and started looking around for an empty spot for us to sit.

"Look, there's Tommy and Peter—" Elizabeth started to say.

"And look who's *with* them," Jessica interrupted her.

At a booth toward the back, Mandy and Lila were sitting with Tommy and Peter. They were laughing at something and looking like they were having the best time. *Uh-oh*, I thought, glancing at the expression on Jessica's face.

"Now I know why they didn't show up to meet us," Jessica said, frowning, her hands on her hips.

"Come on, let's go say hi," Maria said, tugging at Jessica's sleeve. She walked over toward their booth, and I followed her. Lila and Mandy were so wrapped up in their conversation, they didn't even notice us until we were standing right in front of them.

"Hey!" Mandy said. "What's up?"

"Hi, you guys," Maria said. "How's it going?"

"We're in the middle of dissecting a Casey's Super Sundae," Tommy said. He poked at his dish with a spoon. "I think there's, like, a pound of cholesterol in here."

"Not to mention all the fat," Lila added. "That's why I always get lowfat frozen yogurt instead."

"How can you care about what's in a Super Sundae when it tastes so great?" Elizabeth asked. "Don't tell me you're on a diet or something."

Peter shook his head.

"Peter, maybe you could do your next science project on ice cream," Mandy suggested. Peter's a real brain, especially when it comes to science— he's always winning first place at science fairs.

"So," Jessica said casually. "What are *you* guys up to today?"

"We played video games at that store downtown for a while, and then we ate lunch at my house, and now we're killing time before the four o'clock matinee of *Murder Mayday*," Lila said, smiling at Tommy.

"That sounds great," Elizabeth said.

Jessica just glowered for a second, and I saw Elizabeth poke her in the ribs and mouth, "Be nice."

"That does sound like fun. But, um, didn't you *forget* something?" Jessica asked, sounding very sweet and forgiving about the whole thing. I knew she wasn't feeling that way.

"Forget?" Mandy asked.

Jessica held up her Verve bag. "Shopping? One o'clock?"

"Oh," Lila said. Her face fell. "I'm sorry, Jessica. I completely forgot!"

"We were kind of worried, seeing as how you didn't show up or call or anything," Maria said.

"You didn't call?" Mandy asked Lila. "I thought you were going to call Jessica this morning."

Lila winced as if she were anticipating a blow. When nothing happened, she sighed. "I guess I forgot. I'm really sorry," she said without looking up at us.

Jessica raised one eyebrow. "Yeah, I guess you did forget," she said.

Lila turned back to her. "Jessica, I said I was sorry."

Peter cleared his throat. "Hey, do you guys want to go to the movies with us?" he asked in a friendly voice. It was nice of him to try to break the tension. "It starts in about ten minutes, so we should get going."

"No, thanks," Jessica said. "But have a great time." She stared at Lila, but Lila just brushed past her as she got out of the booth, holding Tommy's hand.

We sat down in the booth, and the waiter cleared off the table. "So, um, what do you guys feel like eating?" I asked. I could tell everyone was really bummed, so I tried to lighten the mood a little. "I'm still going for the banana split. Should I get marshmallow *and* whipped cream, just to make it really gross?"

Maria smiled faintly. "No, you might pass out if you eat that. I think I'll just get a small dish of peppermint."

"I want the blueberry pie ice cream," Elizabeth said. "Have you tried that yet, Jessica? It's great. It even has pieces of crust in it."

Jessica shoved the menu away from her. "I'm not hungry," she said.

When she said that, I knew things were even

worse than I'd thought. The last time Jessica wasn't hungry was . . . well, I couldn't even remember a time she wasn't. Things had to be pretty bad, and I had a funny feeling they were only going to get worse.

Five

"Has anyone seen Mary?" Elizabeth asked, walking around the backstage of the auditorium on Monday afternoon.

"I haven't," Maria said, passing through the backstage to the stage to rehearse her next scene.

"Neither have I," I said, as I watched Jessica discussing something with Mr. Drew. "And Mandy's not here, either. We were supposed to meet a half hour ago."

Elizabeth sighed. "I don't know how I'm supposed to get everything ready when nobody's helping."

It's not like Elizabeth to complain—her attitude is usually the more work, the better. She's the most responsible and least whiny person I know. If something was getting on her nerves, then it had to be pretty bad.

I should have known from lunch that day what to expect, I guess. Lately, it seemed that all some of the Unicorns wanted to do was hang out with their new boyfriends, and in the Unicorner it had been the same scene it was on Friday: me, Jessica, Elizabeth, and Maria.

It just wasn't the same without Mandy there to make us laugh, or Ellen there to make a ditsy remark, or Lila to boss us around (even though she doesn't mean to), or Mary to tell us all to calm down and just think rationally. I'd gotten so used to having all my friends there, I really missed it when they weren't. But the way things were going, it looked as if I'd be eating a lot more lunches without all the Unicorns. I'd just have to get used to it. I didn't want Mandy *not* to eat lunch with Peter—I just wanted to spend more time with her. We were supposed to be co-costume designers, but since Thursday she'd hardly done anything.

A few minutes later, Mary ran into the backstage area, all out of breath.

"Where were you?" Elizabeth asked. "Were you out jogging or something?"

Mary shook her head. "No, I ran out to buy this for Rick, for luck." She held up a new dark-green baseball cap, with a big *R* stitched in white on the front.

"Where did you go?" Elizabeth asked. "The mall?"

"No, I went to that sports shop, over by the high school," Mary said.

"How come it took you so long?" Elizabeth asked. "That's only a couple of miles away."

"I couldn't decide which one to get," Mary said. "I think I looked at about two hundred." She turned the baseball cap around in her hand. "So do you think he'll like it?"

Elizabeth shrugged. "Sure, why wouldn't he?" She seemed very irritated.

"I think it's great," I said, nodding. "What team is that from?"

"Some minor-league baseball team from the forties. Pretty cool, huh?" Mary asked.

"Hey, Mary, we don't have a lot of time left today. Do you think you could maybe help me with this?"

"Sure, just a minute, Elizabeth. Rick's on a break right now, and I want to go give the cap to him," Mary said. "I'll be right back, OK?" Then she hurried over to the stage-left wings. Rick had just walked offstage to watch the other cast members rehearse.

"I might as well be working by myself," Elizabeth complained. "Peter's not here because he's doing something with Mandy, and Tommy is over there talking to Lila while she's supposed to be making sure everyone's working!"

"I know," I said. "Well, here comes Mandy." I pointed to the side door. "That means Peter will be here in a second to help you out."

"I'll never finish this backdrop of the amusement-park ride," Elizabeth muttered as I turned to wait for Mandy.

"Evie!" Mandy cried when she saw me. "I am *so* sorry I'm late." She dropped her backpack onto the wooden floor.

"Well, we don't have much time. I need to leave early to get to my lesson," I told her. "Do you want to just take a look at the stuff the seamstress dropped off today?"

"Oh, was it today she was bringing stuff in? I completely forgot." Mandy picked up a dress from the table, where I'd set some of the new items.

Completely forgot? That sounds familiar, I thought. I still hadn't asked Mary and Ellen where they'd been on Saturday, when we were supposed to meet at the mall. I hadn't seen either one of them long enough to actually have a conversation—at least one that didn't revolve one hundred percent around Rick or Tim.

"This is pretty. Jessica's going to look fantastic in this," Mandy said.

"No, that's for Maria, not Jessica," I reminded her. "Remember, Jessica always wears that letter sweater with the *F* on it, for 'Freshman'?"

"Oh, right. Is that done yet?" Mandy asked, looking through the other few things the seamstress had dropped off. Rick's outfits and the costume for the vampire in the amusement park would take the longest to get ready.

"It's already done. We got it at the Attic, remember?" I told her.

"We did?" Mandy asked.

"OK, *I* did, on Saturday afternoon. But we talked about it last week," I said.

"Huh." Mandy looked perplexed, like maybe she thought she was working on some other play.

"Mandy, come here for a second. You have to see what I just painted!" Peter called from behind a large piece of backdrop.

"I've got work to do, Peter!" Mandy yelled back. "Can't I look at it later?"

"Come on, Mandy, you *have* to see this. It's really funny," Peter added. "I made a major mistake and I need to paint over it in a second."

"Well . . . OK. Sorry, Evie. I'll be right back, I promise. Then we can go through the rest of these," Mandy said, and she walked over to Peter.

Sure you will, I thought, but it didn't matter, because I had to take off for my lesson anyway. At least the job of costume designer wasn't too much work. Otherwise, I thought, we might be in big trouble. The first performance was barely two weeks away.

"Isn't it great to be going somewhere besides the auditorium or the art studio?" Elizabeth asked me as we walked into the day-care center on Tuesday after school. She, Jessica, Maria, and I had just ridden our bikes over together. Since the other four Unicorns usually—as of the last week, anyway—met up with their boyfriends after school, we'd just mentioned that we were going when we passed them on the school steps. They'd promised to show up in just a few minutes.

"Jessica!" Oliver Washington, true to form, threw down a coloring book and charged straight at Jessica, plowing into her knees.

She hugged him and said, "Hey, Oliver. Boy, have I missed you."

"You haven't been here in forever," Oliver complained.

"I know. But we told you, we're working on a big play at school. We have to rehearse it almost every afternoon, so it'll be ready soon," Jessica explained.

"Are there any parts in it for little girls?" Sandy Meyer asked.

Her twin, Allison, who's a favorite of Elizabeth's, nodded. "Yeah, can we be in it?"

"Well . . . I don't think so, Allie," Elizabeth said. "I don't know if there's anything you can do in this play."

"I was in a play in school last year," Arthur Foo announced.

"Really? What did you do?" I asked him.

"I was a carrot," Arthur said.

"So you've really got some acting experience," Maria teased, smiling at him. "Well, maybe your class will do another play this year."

"All they ever do at school is boring stuff with Ben Franklin and Thomas Jefferson and junk like that," Arthur complained. "It's supposed to be fun, but it isn't."

"Hey, I have an idea," Jessica said. "Why don't we get you guys some tickets to our play, and you can come watch it? It's going to be a *lot* more fun than some old history play."

"What's it about?" Yuky asked.

"Well, it's got a vampire in it, for one thing," I told her.

"Vampires are so cool," Oliver said. "I want to be a vampire when I grow up."

"No, you don't," Jessica said. "You'd have to grow some really hideous fangs, for one thing." She bared her teeth at him, and he shrieked and took off running. She chased him around the room, and he squealed as he darted around a corner and hid behind the kitchen cabinets.

The Center's pretty well equipped, considering they don't have a lot of money. Mrs. Willard really knows how to organize things. And in addition to the money that the city of Sweet Valley gives to the Center, she gets donations from people and companies in town to cover extra things. The Unicorn Club has even pitched in to raise the money to build a new roof—Maria donated the money she earned from acting in *Secondhand Rose* for that. And we've done a bunch of things to make the playroom more fun, including donating old board games we had at home and putting up lots of bright posters the kids made. There's a kitchen with snack supplies, like peanut butter and crackers—nothing fancy. And outside is a playground with a jungle gym, for when everyone gets really hyper, which is practically all the time.

"Evie, are you in the play?" Yuky asked me as I went into the kitchen to pour her and Sandy glasses of milk.

"No," I said. "But I am involved, because Mandy and I are choosing what everyone in the play will wear."

"Where is Mandy?" Yuky asked.

"Yeah, and where's Lila?" Ellie McMillan asked. I hadn't noticed her at first. She was lying on one of the big pillows over by the window, reading a picture book. Ellie's the girl I told you about whom Lila really hit it off with, and they usually spend a lot of time together.

I looked at the clock above the sink. "They should be here soon. They said they'd be over in a couple of minutes—"

"And that was half an hour ago," Jessica said, finishing the sentence for me.

"Well, they'll probably be here soon," I told Ellie.

"I wouldn't count on it," Jessica grumbled. Then she started helping Oliver with some of his homework.

I played Chutes and Ladders with Yuky, Sandy, Allison, and Elizabeth. It's their favorite board game, and they always insist we play whenever we're there. It's fine, if you can get through the game without Allison and Sandy having a major blowout. Maria was doing some painting with

Arthur, who's really very talented when it comes to art.

Sandy was two squares from the finish line of our first game when Ellen rushed into the room, panting. "You guys, I am *so* sorry," she apologized. She came over to the table and ruffled Yuky's hair. "How are you doing? Hi, Arthur!" she called.

"I'm OK." Yuky shrugged. I could tell she felt a little insulted that Ellen was so late. It was four thirty, and in an hour the parents would start coming in to pick the kids up.

"Come over and look at what I'm painting!" Arthur called to Ellen.

"I'll be there in a second," Ellen promised.

"What happened to you?" Jessica asked. "And where's everyone else?"

"How should I know?" Ellen replied. She walked over to the kitchen counter and took an apple out of the basket of fruit Mrs. Willard put out every week. "I really didn't mean to be late, but since Mr. Drew gave us the afternoon off and everything, Tim and I wanted to do something special together, so we went to the video arcade and played a bunch of games. Of course, he won almost every time."

"Who's Tim?" Yuky asked.

"My boyfriend," Ellen said.

"Yuck!" Allison said, making a face as she moved her game piece down a chute.

"Is he cute?" Sandy asked. "Does he look like

Sam Smith from that California surfing show?"

"No, he has brown hair," Ellen said. Just thinking about Tim seemed to send her off into deep space. She had this really vacant look on her face. You know the expression "stars in her eyes"?

"Ellen and Tim, sittin' in a tree," Arthur started chanting.

"K-I-S-S-I-N-G!" everyone yelled in unison, and then they laughed and started chanting it again. Ellen blushed and laughed.

"She comes over here to see the kids and all she can talk about is Tim," Jessica grumbled to me as we started cleaning up the play area, putting crayons and papers away. "As if they care about that stuff."

"I know," I said. "All the girls think boys are disgusting, and all the boys think girls have cooties."

"Not to mention the fact that she got here ten minutes before quitting time," Jessica said, exaggerating.

The kids' parents started arriving at a little before five thirty. We said good-bye to each of the kids and promised we'd be back sooner than the last time. I could see how much it meant to everyone that we'd been there, and I vowed I'd be back at least once more that week.

Ellie's mother was the last one to show up, and we all waited with Ellie until she did. Ellie was being uncharacteristically quiet. She hadn't budged from her spot on the floor in hours, the whole time we were there, except to go to the bathroom.

"Ellie, are you OK?" Jessica asked, sitting beside her on the floor. "I mean, are you feeling sick or anything?"

"I'm OK," Ellie said, closing her book.

"Are you sure?" I asked. "You can talk to us about anything, you know."

Ellie played with her sock, rolling it up and back. "How come Lila's not here?"

"Well . . . she must have had something important to do," Jessica said.

"Like what?" Ellie asked.

"I don't know," Jessica said. "Maybe she had an extra homework assignment or something like that."

I admired the way Jessica was handling the situation. Even though she was angry at Lila for not showing up, she wasn't going to let Ellie see that. "Yeah, or maybe she had to do some work on the play," I added.

Ellie looked up at us. Her face was so sad, I thought she was going to start crying. "Doesn't she like me anymore?" she asked.

"Of course she does," Jessica said, wrapping her arm around Ellie's shoulder. "Lila's crazy about you—you know that."

"Yeah, I *know* she wanted to come today," I said. "Ellie, Lila really cares about you. I'm sure something came up that she couldn't get out of."

"You know what? I'm going to talk to Lila tonight," Jessica said. "Maybe I can get her to come by tomorrow and see you. How would that be?"

Ellie nodded. "Good."

"And if she can't come to see you, I'll tell her she should call you, OK?" Jessica asked, just as Mrs. McMillan walked into the room.

"OK!" Ellie jumped up and ran over to her mother, giving her a big hug. The two of them said good-bye and left, and we locked the door and followed them down the hall.

"Did you see how upset she was?" Jessica commented to Elizabeth as we went outside.

"Lila will have to make it up to her somehow," Elizabeth said. "That's all there is to it."

We were unlocking our bikes when Mandy coasted up. "Oh, no. What time is it?" she asked when she saw us.

"Ten to six," Maria said. "You missed it."

"By a long shot," Jessica added.

Mandy seemed a little taken aback by Jessica's tone. "Well, I got here as soon as I could, after Peter and I finished our science project together. Peter's great at science—it took me half the time it would have if I'd only worked on it myself. We thought we should take advantage of the afternoon off from rehearsal and get ahead on our homework," she said.

"But we were all supposed to be here, for the kids," Elizabeth said. "Didn't we remind you of that, like, two hours ago?"

"Oh. Well, I guess so," Mandy said. "I'm sorry. I guess I figured with everyone else here, no one would really miss me."

"Well, you really hurt the kids' feelings," Jessica said. "Everyone was asking where you were."

"Oh, no. I feel awful. Well, I'll just have to make it up to them somehow. I'll come by in a couple of days by myself," Mandy said breezily. "Hey, Ellen, do you and Tim want to go out with me and Peter on Thursday for pizza?"

The two of them started talking, and Jessica, Elizabeth, Maria, and I started pedaling slowly down the street toward home. I didn't know about everyone else, but I was thinking Mandy needed to make it up to *us*, too—not just the kids. Lately she and Ellen had been acting as if we were practically invisible. This wasn't the first plan they'd broken with us, and I had a feeling it wasn't going to be the last.

But what could we do about it? They had new boyfriends, and they wanted to spend all their time with them. And we were just going to have to get used to it.

Six

That night nobody called me. Usually Mary does, or Mandy, and sometimes Maria. (It's kind of confusing having my best friends' names all start with the same letter, I know.) Anyway, it made me feel kind of odd. No, maybe sad is more like it. Since I've been a member of the Unicorns, we've had some problems getting along, like when we went on a local game show called *Best Friends*. We lost, and we all stopped speaking to one another for a couple of days.

But this felt different. I couldn't really be angry at anyone, because they hadn't done anything wrong exactly. I just felt that maybe our club was changing, and not for the better. Of course, I was happy for my friends. I wanted them to be happy. I just didn't want to feel as left out as I did. And because everyone was already a year older than I was, it seemed that it was only going to be more and more like that, as soon as everyone got boyfriends.

But I couldn't say anything. It would seem that I was whining, and I absolutely hate people who whine, because usually they're upset about tiny, little things. They have no idea what it's like to be *really* down in the dumps. I decided I'd just wait and see whether things changed. If my friends wanted to see their boyfriends more than me, then I'd just have to get used to it, even if I didn't like it.

The next morning in Spanish class, Jessica didn't waste any time telling Lila how *she* felt about the whole thing. "Lila, Ellie was really upset that you didn't show up yesterday," Jessica said. "You should call her."

"Oh, I'm sure I'll see her this weekend or something," Lila said with a shrug. "And if I don't, I'll call and see how she's doing." She took out a notebook and set it on her desk.

"So why didn't you show up?" Jessica asked. "It was pretty irresponsible of you, you know. Those kids depend on us."

"What are you, doing your Mrs. Willard imitation?" Lila scoffed. "So I didn't make it—it's not mandatory. What's the big deal?"

"It is a big deal when you promise to do something with someone and then you blow it off," Jessica said. "Especially when it's little kids."

I watched them from my seat in the third row, too nervous to join the conversation. When Jessica and Lila argue, it can get pretty intense.

"Were you doing something with Tommy instead?" Jessica continued.

"Yeah. We went over to his house and I met his brother and his two sisters," Lila said. "They're really nice. Just like him."

"Well, that's great, but you were supposed to be meeting *us*," Jessica said.

"I know," Lila admitted with a sigh. "And I feel bad about not being there. But . . . I don't know. I just can't help it, Jessica. It seemed more important to hang out with Tommy and his family," Lila said with a shrug. "Maybe it wasn't the best decision, but that's what I did. I'll make it up to Ellie, I promise."

"That's what you say now, but the next time we do something, are you going to blow that off, too?" Jessica asked.

"Look, Jessica," Lila said angrily. "I'm tired of you yelling at me. I haven't done anything wrong! You just don't understand what it's like with me and Tommy. I want to spend every possible minute with him. You have no idea how—"

"You're right, I don't," Jessica said, and with that she went to sit at her desk, two rows behind Lila.

I ate lunch with Maria and Elizabeth—now even Jessica wasn't in the Unicorner. She was nowhere to be found.

"I think she must be working on memorizing her lines in the library or something," Elizabeth said. "She said something last night about how she was so upset, she couldn't focus."

"Maybe I can help her this afternoon," Maria said. "I know some good techniques. But to tell you the truth, I can't imagine how we'll ever pull off this play. Ellen's so distracted by Tim that she can't see straight. How's she ever going to be ready for opening night in two weeks?"

"I don't know, but she has to be," Elizabeth said. "We're not putting in all this work for it to be a flop."

"Mr. Drew told me that the ticket committee has sold almost all the tickets for opening night already," Maria said.

"You're kidding! How?" I asked.

"They called all the parents and advertised in the *Tribune*," Maria said. "I guess everyone's so excited because it's Mr. Drew's own play, and he does have a great reputation."

"Well, I think it's because *you're* in it," I said to Maria, and smiled.

"Thank you, thank you," Maria said, taking a phony bow.

I laughed and then, out of the corner of my eye, I saw Rick, Tim, Ellen, and Mary sitting at a table close by. Some other people were sitting there, too, kids I didn't know. Mostly eighth graders. Mary and Ellen were talking and laughing with them, too. I just stared at them for a second, even though I felt really hurt. They hadn't eaten lunch with us once all week, and now here they were, making a whole new group of friends.

"So . . . has anyone talked to Mary in the last couple of days?" I asked Elizabeth and Maria.

Maria shook her head. "Not even to say boo to."

"Just at rehearsal, and then only for a second," Elizabeth said. "I wonder how she's doing."

"Me, too," I said. "I don't know. Things are pretty weird when the most practical and sensible person you know starts going off the deep end about some guy."

"Rick is a great guy," Maria said. "I mean, I guess if I were in her place, maybe I'd be acting that way, too."

"Yeah, I guess. It's hard for me to imagine being so in love," I admitted.

"I've had major crushes before," Maria said, "but they never turned into anything."

We all sat there for a minute and just gazed over at their table. I don't know what Elizabeth and Maria were thinking, but I was thinking that on the one hand, I'd love to be in their shoes, but on the other, I'd rather stay right where I was.

Jessica came into the cafeteria toward the end of lunch period. I saw her glance at where Lila was sitting with Tommy and his friends. Then she just walked right past her, without even saying hello.

She came over to the Unicorner table and slammed her science book down.

"I'm sorry, but that is the absolute limit," she fumed.

"What is? Sit down," Elizabeth said.

"OK. Lila and I were supposed to get together for half our lunch period, because we're working on that science project together, and we've fallen way behind because of the play. So I'm sitting up in the lab, missing lunch, starving to death, and she's down here!" Jessica exclaimed, practically all in one breath. "And now there's not even enough time for me to eat!"

"Here, have some cookies." I pushed my tray toward her.

"Maybe she—" Elizabeth began.

"Don't tell me she forgot." Jessica bit into a cookie, sending crumbs flying. "Don't even say that to me. That's all I ever hear lately. Besides, we only made the plan this morning in science class, when Mr. Siegel got on our case for being late with it!"

"Maybe it's a case of short-term memory loss?" Maria suggested with a half smile.

Jessica took another bite and a chocolate chip fell onto the table. She quickly swept it off onto the floor. "I've had it with her. She can do her dumb project with Mr. Wonderful, for all I care. See how well she does. She'll probably be gazing into his eyes and spill hydrochloric acid on her stupid silk shirt."

I couldn't help laughing at that. Jessica glared at

me. "I'm sorry, Jessica. I know it's not funny."

"Look, we're all tired of being blown off for their boyfriends. It's not just Lila," Maria said. "I mean, I might even expect it of her and Ellen, but not Mary and Mandy."

"Well, I think it's time for us to *do* something about it," Jessica said.

"Like what?" Elizabeth asked. "I mean, we can't exactly tell them not to have boyfriends."

"Besides, they're really in love," I said.

"In love or not," Jessica said, "they still should be our friends. And the way I see it, they have one more chance to prove whether or not they're really our friends."

"What do you mean?" Elizabeth asked.

"I think we should offer to have a Unicorn meeting at our house on Friday night," Jessica said. "A combination meeting and party. And we should see who comes to that."

"If it's an official Unicorn meeting, then everyone has to come, right?" I asked. "Unless they're sick or something."

"Right," Jessica said. "And being lovesick is not an excuse."

"So what are you saying? They either come, or they're out?" Elizabeth asked. "That seems kind of harsh."

"Look, if they come, no big deal—we'll all have a great time and it'll be good to catch up with everyone again," Maria said.

Jessica nodded. "And if they don't come . . . well, then we'll have to decide what happens next."

That had a pretty ominous sound to it, but who wouldn't come to an official meeting? Maria was right. It would be just the thing to patch things up between all of us and get things back to normal. Unicorn normal, anyway.

The next morning, Thursday, the four of us met out on the steps leading up to school. We'd decided to ask them then, because it was the one time we knew we could get everyone together in the same place without trying too hard (everyone *had* to show up for school). We spotted Mandy and Lila right away—they weren't heading toward us, naturally, but toward Peter and Tommy. It was like the front steps were divided into sections: kids in couples, and kids not in couples. Mary walked up the sidewalk a minute later and went right over to Rick, who was talking to Tim, who was standing next to Ellen.

"Everyone's here. Let's go," Jessica said.

She sounded so serious, kind of like a cop in a television movie. I looked nervously at Elizabeth. I don't know why, but I didn't have a very good feeling about this. Maybe it was because Jessica was acting as if she were a general, leading us into battle.

"Hi, you guys," Elizabeth said politely when we got over to them.

"Hi!" Mary said. She sounded excited to see us.

"How've you been?" Mandy asked. "I haven't seen you guys in practically forever."

"No kidding," Jessica said.

Maria cleared her throat. "Yeah, it's good to see you, too. Hey, do you think we could talk to you for a minute?" She jerked her head to the side. "You know, over there. Alone."

"Oh." Ellen looked at Tim. "Well, OK, for a minute, anyway."

We all moved away from the group of couples to a shady spot underneath one of the big elm trees by the sidewalk.

"Look, what Mandy said is right. We haven't seen you guys in forever," Elizabeth said. "I mean, not really."

"We wanted to tell you that we're going to have a meeting at our house tomorrow night," Jessica said. "Part meeting, part party. We'll order some pizzas, get lots of ice cream, and make sundaes, rent some movies, whatever. You should come over around seven o'clock."

"How does that sound?" Maria asked.

Mary brushed a leaf out of her hair. "Friday night?" she asked. "Like, um, *tomorrow* night?"

"That's what I said—tomorrow night," Jessica said. "Is that a problem?"

"Well, I don't know. Tommy said something about taking me to a soccer game," Lila said. "It's kind of a big deal because they're some Italian team on tour."

"And Rick and I already made plans to have dinner with his family," Mary said. "I don't think I can get out of it."

"Yeah, and Peter and I are renting that new concert video of the Bashers with his older brother and some of his friends," Mandy said. "It's kind of already set."

"What about you, Ellen?" Jessica asked. "Do *you* have plans, too?"

"Of course," Ellen said. "I mean, it is a Friday night. Actually, we'll probably do something really romantic. It's our one-week anniversary."

Jessica rolled her eyes. "Didn't you guys hear me say that this was an *official* Unicorn meeting?"

Lila looked at her and shrugged. "So?"

"So, you should be there!" Jessica replied. "Isn't that one of the rules we made?"

"Well, maybe it was a rule in the past," Mary said. "But—"

"But nothing," Jessica said. "It's not like we can change the rules for you just because you feel like it."

"I didn't say to change the rules for me!" Mary protested. "It's just that maybe we should make allowances for things that didn't come up before."

"Make allowances? Make allowances?" Jessica repeated. "That's all I've been doing lately, and I'm getting really tired of it. This week you guys have ditched every single plan we tried to make with you. And now you won't even come to a meeting."

"Look, Jessica, I don't want to argue with you,"

Mary said. "But come on. I've never had a real boy-friend before, not like Rick, anyway. Can't we just make plans for next week?"

"No, we can't," Jessica said. "We need to have a meeting tomorrow, and that's why we called it. If you guys can't make it, then—"

"Well, Jessica." Lila flipped her hair over her shoulder and glanced behind her, toward where Tommy was. "You might find this hard to believe, but sometimes there are more important things in life than having a little meeting."

"A little meeting?" Jessica retorted. "So that's all it means to you?"

"Look, I'm sorry, but Lila's right," Ellen said. "Sometimes there are more important things than doing every little thing together with your friends."

"Oh, really?" Maria said.

"So spending time with your boyfriends is more important than spending time with us?" Elizabeth asked. "Do you actually mean that?"

"You guys don't understand," Mary said quietly.

"No, *you* don't understand," Jessica said. "Either you want to be our friends, and be Unicorns, or you don't. And if you don't come to that meeting tomorrow night, then I guess you don't want to be Unicorns anymore!"

"Well, if being a Unicorn means we have to spend every single second with you, then maybe you're right!" Mandy said.

"If it's such a pain being a Unicorn, then you

should quit!" Jessica said. "We sure wouldn't want to make your lives terrible by making you hang out with us."

"If our friendship isn't worth anything to you, then let's just forget about having a club," Elizabeth said.

"Good!" Ellen said. "Now I can go to the movies with Tim!"

"Fine!" Jessica said. "Have fun!"

Mandy, Lila, Ellen, and Mary all turned and walked away. The bell rang to start school, but I couldn't move. I just stood there, watching them walk into school with their boyfriends. I couldn't believe it. We'd given them a choice—us or them—and they'd chosen *them*.

The Unicorn Club didn't exist anymore. My new best friends didn't want any part of it.

I didn't know what to do or what to say. I felt a tear slide down my cheek.

"It's OK, Evie," Elizabeth said to me. "We can still be good friends.

"Yeah, and at least we know the meaning of friendship," Maria said.

"I bet we'll be even better friends now," Jessica said. She put her arm around my shoulders and we started walking up the steps. "We're better off without them," she said, but her voice was shaky, and I knew, deep down, she didn't really believe that any more than I did.

Seven

"You can sit there if you want to, but I'm not going to," Jessica declared to me when we walked into the cafeteria together that noon. "In fact, I don't even want to see anything with a unicorn on it, and I can't wait until I get home so I can change out of this purple shirt."

Four hours after our fight, it was as if the Unicorn Club had dissolved into thin air. We sat at a little table in the middle of the cafeteria. About halfway through lunch, I noticed a few kids sitting over in what used to be the Unicorner. They looked completely out of place. I almost went over there and told them to get lost. Couldn't they respect our space and let us have it empty for just one day, in memory of the club? *Well, I guess it's anybody's table now,* I thought. *It's not like we'll be needing it back anytime soon.*

Partway through lunch, I went back into the line to get a refill on my glass of apple juice. I practically bumped right into Mary as I angled over to the drinks machine.

"Excuse me," I said. I reached my arm in to press the juice button.

Mary just stood there and waited until I was done before she made another move. I looked her right in the eye, thinking maybe that if I was really nice, she'd break down and apologize. She just stared past me as if I weren't even there.

Then she turned to some girls I didn't know. I'd seen her with them over the past week. I guess they were Rick's friends' girlfriends. "Did you guys see that new Johnny Buck video last night?"

"The premiere, you mean? Oh, that was so cool," one of the other girls said. "I'd give anything to see him in concert."

"I've seen him—five times," Mary said.

"Wow! That's a ton," another girl said. "Did you have good seats?"

I didn't stick around to hear any more. I knew all about Mary's obsession with the rock star Johnny Buck, and I was used to her talking to the Unicorns about it. By the time I got back to the table, I was so nervous and upset that I was shaking. "I ran into Mary," I told Jessica.

"What did she say?" Jessica asked.

"Nothing," I said. "Not even 'Excuse me.'"

Jessica poked at her pasta salad. "Well, that figures. I used to think Mary was the nicest person on earth. Not anymore."

I just shrugged. I didn't know what to think about *anyone* anymore.

"That wasn't such a bad quiz," Elizabeth said. "I thought it would be harder." It was Friday, and we had just finished our algebra test. I don't have too many classes with the seventh graders, but I'm pretty advanced in some subjects, like English and math, so they let me into seventh-grade classes for those. (I used to go to a pretty fancy private school in Los Angeles, which is why I'm ahead.) And Spanish is based on language ability, not on grade year. In each foreign-language class, there's a mix of grades.

"Yeah, I'm pretty sure I got them all, except maybe that last word problem," I said.

"Uh-oh," Elizabeth suddenly said. We were on the way to our lockers to get our books for our next class, and coming down the hall toward us were Mandy and Lila—for once, without Tim and Tommy.

When she was a few yards away, Mandy looked at me and then deliberately turned to Lila and started laughing about something. Lila gave Elizabeth a glance, then held her head up even higher in the air, as if she were the queen of Sweet Valley Middle School or something.

"Oh, please," I muttered to Elizabeth right after they had passed us. "Who do they think they are?"

"I don't know, but this school is starting to feel pretty small," Elizabeth said. "We're going to run into one another all over the place."

"No kidding," I said. "Maybe it'll get better after a little while."

"I don't know about you, but I'm still pretty upset," Elizabeth said. "I don't think they were right, but it still feels bad not to talk to them."

"I know," I said. "And I have a question. How are we all supposed to work on the play together when we can't even speak to one another?"

We'd been playing basketball all week in gym. Pretty exciting, right? But there's a point to this. Number one, even though I'm short, I'm really pretty good, especially at bringing the ball up the court. Number two, I happen to have the worst people in that class, and the person on the top of that list is Amanda Harmon. Amanda's an eighth grader who made our lives miserable when we were on that game show, *Best Friends*. We lost to Amanda and her club, the Eight Times Eight Club.

First, Amanda and the Eights (as they are called) started trying to prove how much better than us they were. They were competing with us constantly. Then, when we got selected for *Best Friends*, Amanda made sure the Eights got to go up against us. She bragged all over school about how they were going to trounce us on the show. Then they actually did.

Anyway, we'd made a bet with them that the losers had to sing "Puff the Magic Dragon" in the cafeteria the day after the show. We thought we were going to die of embarrassment, but then we turned "Puff" into a rap song and did a totally hip performance of it that everyone loved. Amanda was so mad at us, she practically breathed fire when we passed her in the hallway for the whole following week.

Anyway, back to basketball. Ellen was also in my class, which was especially awkward. What was worse was that ever since she'd started seeing Tim, she all of a sudden thought she knew a lot about basketball just because he plays really well. I guess she believes in osmosis—that if she hung around him, it'd just rub off onto her. But the truth was, she out-and-out stank at basketball, and I'm not just saying that because of our big fight. She double-dribbled so often, she could make it into the Basketball Hall of Fame just for that.

Ms. Langberg put me and Ellen on the same team that afternoon—naturally. Just to make things even harder. And Amanda was on our team, too. She knows as much about basketball as I do about nuclear physics.

"Now, remember," Ms. Langberg told us all before we headed onto the court for a scrimmage. "The big thing you need to do out there is communicate."

Oh, great, I thought. Since I played point guard, I was the one who had to initiate the plays and communicate with everyone about where to go.

I got the in-bounds pass and started dribbling

up the floor. When I got past half-court, I tossed the ball to Amanda. She passed it to Ellen, and I called a play we'd already used about a hundred times that week. She was supposed to pass it back to me, I'd get it to Carmen, and she'd do a layup.

But Ellen wouldn't pass the ball to me. "Ellen!" I called to her, waving my hands in the air. She just kept it and started moving toward the basket herself, like she was going to score a basket. Someone stole the ball from her in about two seconds, and the other team scored a quick two points.

The same thing happened the next time we had the ball. And the next. Whenever Ellen was supposed to pass to me, she wouldn't. Talk about immature. It wasn't as if I were loving playing with her, either, but at least I could try to make the best of it. Now what? Was I supposed to flunk gym, all because of her?

"You guys are playing terribly," Ms. Langberg said when we took our first time-out. "What's the problem?"

Ellen folded her arms over her chest and glared at me. Nobody else said anything.

"Well, it looks like I'd better make some substitutions," she said. "Ellen and Carmen, you two take a break."

Ellen huffed as she walked over to sit on the bleachers. I wanted to say, "It serves you right, you ball hog!" but I decided that wouldn't be very mature, either.

"Are you guys not talking to each other? What's the deal?" Amanda asked when we went back onto the court.

"I don't want to talk about it," I said. The last thing I needed was Amanda Harmon knowing about the Unicorns' split. She'd probably throw a party to celebrate.

I was dreading that afternoon's rehearsal like you wouldn't believe. Well, maybe you would.

When I got there, I was amazed to see Mandy sitting in a chair backstage by herself, sewing some buttons onto a black leather jacket for one of Rick's scenes. I looked at the clipboard hanging on the wall, where each department had lists of what they needed to have ready. Mandy and I had been checking off things that were already done. I went over to the costume trunk and grabbed the cape my grandmother had lent us. We were sewing some reflecting moons and stars onto it, so they'd show up in dim stage lighting in that scene.

I sat down across from Mandy and started putting the patches on. A minute later, a note slid across the floor to me. My heart started beating faster when I picked it up. Was she going to apologize, already? I wondered.

"Please don't sew all of those on," it said in Mandy's handwriting. I glanced over at her, but she didn't look up.

I took a pen out my pocket and wrote "Why

not?" and shoved the index card back across the floor to her.

"Because I want to make sure it's done right," Mandy wrote back.

"I'm as good at sewing as you are," I wrote. "Don't worry, it'll look fine." I started to sew again, but after all the note shoving, it made me uncomfortable to sit there across from Mandy. I took the cape and started wandering around, looking for another place to work.

First I went over to where Elizabeth and the rest of her crew were painting backdrops. I got there just in time to see Elizabeth and Mary trying to get along. They weren't doing any better than Mandy and I were, and maybe even worse.

"Carmen, could you do me a favor? Could you please tell Mary she needs to finish painting that bat by tomorrow," Elizabeth said to Carmen.

Carmen shrugged and turned to Mary. "Elizabeth wants you to paint that bat today."

"Really?" Mary said. "Tell Elizabeth I think *she* should paint it if she wants it done so quickly. And while you're at it, tell her she's not my boss!"

I couldn't remember ever hearing Mary say something so angrily before. And I couldn't think of a time when Elizabeth had seemed so mad, either.

"Maybe I'm not her boss, Carmen, but somebody around here has to take some initiative or nothing's ever going to get done, because some people haven't done any work at all yet!" Elizabeth retorted.

I wandered up front to get away from that argument. Rick and Ellen were onstage, rehearsing one of the key scenes. It was where Rick (Victor) first meets Ellen (Mallory) and tries to be suave and kiss her. I was surprised Mary wasn't out there to watch Rick, since it seemed she hadn't missed a take yet. Jessica was there, too. I remembered her telling me that she usually helped Ellen with her lines a bit, since she was in almost every scene as the Freshman.

" 'It's nice to meet you,' " Ellen said.

" 'Likewise.' " Rick held out his hand, and when Ellen shook it, he leaned down and pressed his lips against her hand.

" 'Easy,' " Jessica said. " 'She doesn't like to be kissed on first dates.' "

Rick looked over his shoulder at Jessica. " 'Who are you, anyway? I've seen you everywhere ever since I got to town.' "

" 'Me? I'm nobody. Just a freshman,' " Jessica said with a shrug. " 'Well, gotta go—see ya!' " She dashed across the stage to the other side, where she'd be hidden behind the curtain when the play was actually on.

Ellen looked after her with a kind of panicked expression. I guess Jessica really had been helping Ellen by hanging out and prompting her with lines. Ellen pushed her hair back behind her ears, and then she seemed to regain her control.

" 'So tell me about yourself, Mallory.' " Rick sat down on one of the folding chairs on the stage. It would be replaced by a restaurant booth for the production. "'I want to know everything about you.'"

"'Everything?'" Ellen asked.

Rick nodded. "'The good and the bad.'"

Ellen smiled nervously. "'I'm not sure what to tell you. I love old movies like *Casabonita*—'"

"*Casablanca*," Mr. Drew hissed. "Casa Bonita is a restaurant." He was standing off to the side of the stage, shaking his head.

"'I love old movies like *Casablanca*, I'm a Sagittarius—'"

"Aquarius," Mr. Drew corrected. "Where is Lila, anyway? She's supposed to feed you lines when you get stuck."

Ellen shrugged. "I'm not sure where she is."

"I think she's back checking out the sets," Rick said.

"Or filing her nails," Jessica added with a frown.

"Well, I'm going to find her. You two continue, because I won't be out of earshot," Mr. Drew instructed. "Come on, Ellen—think."

Ellen sighed. "'I'm an Aquarius, which means I love water, and that's funny, because I'm on the swim team.'" She paused, waiting for Rick to say something. She turned to him hopefully, but he shook his head.

"This is your big monologue, remember?" he said. "You've still got another five minutes to go. You get all dreamy about your plans for the future and all that, and I get so wrapped up in the moment that I kiss you."

"Right." Ellen's face turned pink. "How could I forget that?"

I bet she was glad Tim was off rehearsing his scene in another room. I guess I learned one important thing that afternoon. You really can't learn in your sleep after all.

Eight

"Somehow this isn't quite how I pictured it." Elizabeth slid a party pizza into the oven. When you only have four people for a party, there's not much point in ordering pizzas, is there? Instead we'd raided the Wakefields' refrigerator.

"Just because there are only four of us doesn't mean we can't have fun," Jessica declared, pouring four glasses of grapefruit soda.

"Jessica's right. I mean, we've had tons of fun by ourselves before," Maria added.

"And we definitely don't need any boys around," I said.

"That's for sure," Jessica said, putting the soda back into the refrigerator.

"So what movies did you get?" Elizabeth asked Maria.

"OK. Don't get mad, because I got four, and if there's one you don't like we don't have to watch it," Maria said. "But I thought if all of us were here it would be fun if we had kind of a Dracula-vampire marathon."

"That's a great idea!" Jessica said enthusiastically.

"They kind of range from the original black-and-white *Dracula* to the modern blood-and-gore." Maria held up a cassette case. "Plus I got a copy of *Summer Surf*, in case we get sick of bats."

I laughed. "Yeah, I don't know how many times I can watch that part where Dracula turns into a bat."

Jessica put her hands out to the side and pretended to be flapping her wings as she moved around the kitchen. "Maybe your part should be the Flying Rodent instead of the Freshman," Maria joked, and Jessica deliberately ran into her.

We picked up a couple of the pizzas and our drinks and went into the living room. Mr. and Mrs. Wakefield had gone out to a movie and were coming back at nine, and Elizabeth and Jessica's brother Steven was on a date.

I love hanging out at the Wakefields' house, because it's pretty big and it's really comfortable. Plus they somehow always make you feel like it's your house, too.

We sat down and started eating. After a couple of minutes, things seemed kind of awkward.

"So are we having a meeting?" I asked nervously.

"Well, I guess there's no point having a meeting

first, if we're not Unicorns anymore," Elizabeth said.

"Are *we* not Unicorns, or is it just everyone else?" Maria asked.

Jessica set her glass down on the coffee table. "Here's what I think. I think we should start a new club."

"What?" all three of us practically cried at once.

"Sure, why not?" Jessica asked, as if it were the most logical idea in the world.

"I don't know about the rest of you, but I don't feel like starting a new club right away," Elizabeth said. "For one thing, the Unicorn Club was great—"

"While it lasted," Jessica finished for her. "Which it didn't."

"True," Maria said. "But . . . I don't know. I don't think we should rush into anything."

"Why not? Don't tell me you think we're actually going to get back together with them. You guys don't think that's going to happen, do you?" Jessica asked.

Nobody said anything. I guess that's what we were all hoping, in a way, even if it was unrealistic.

"Well, it's not," Jessica said. "I mean, even if they wanted to, why should we forget everything they did? They said we didn't matter to them anymore, remember?"

We all nodded. It was kind of like Jessica was our coach, and she was revving us up for our next game. Either our coach, or a talk-show host. Half of what we were saying sounded like something a divorced couple might say. But the situation wasn't much different, really. We had been separated. And Jessica was right—unless something drastic happened, we probably weren't getting back together. You couldn't take back the things we'd all said the day before, outside school.

"Let's not make up a new club yet," Elizabeth said. "It just doesn't feel right."

Jessica leaned back on the couch. "OK, if you say so. But we might as well start thinking about it. It's not like I'm ever going to wear my Unicorn jacket again."

Tom Sanders, the director of *Secondhand Rose*, had given us all jackets with our names on them, as thanks for helping when he made the movie in Sweet Valley. Mine had been hanging in my closet for the past week, ever since things started getting weird. The night before, I had hidden it in the back, behind all my sweaters, so I wouldn't have to look at it and feel even worse.

We didn't have such a great time on Friday night, but I was glad we'd gotten together. I spent the weekend at home, and at the Attic with my grandmother. It was nice to see more of her, and I know it means a lot to her when we can do stuff together. We always try to spend Sundays together.

But since the club wasn't doing anything as a group anymore, I felt as if I had a lot of free time— too much free time, actually. Some people think that's impossible, but I don't. I get really tired of doing the same things all the time: homework, violin lessons and practice, and the play.

I guess it was fortunate Mandy and I—with the help of the seamstress Mr. Drew hired—were almost completely done with our part in the play. (Of course, we'd be there during the performances to make sure everyone kept their outfits straight.) I was glad. At the moment, I couldn't handle seeing Mandy any more than I absolutely had to—or seeing Mary, Ellen, or Lila and not talking to them.

At least I still had Elizabeth. We'd always gotten along pretty well, even though I was closer to Mandy and Maria. The club breakup had given me a chance to get to know her better.

Elizabeth and I were hanging out in the school library during fourth-period study hall on Monday when we overheard the president of the Eights, Amanda Harmon, talking to one of her best friends, Kristin Benson, who's also a member of the Eights. Amanda was sitting at a table on the other side of the stacks from where we were, so she had no idea we were there. I recognized her voice right away—in addition to being mean and obnoxious, she's also incredibly loud. I guess that goes with the territory.

Amanda and Kristin were talking about the semiformal dance, which was scheduled for the weekend right after the play. "Mr. Clark told me there really is going to be a band," Kristin said.

"For a semiformal? Really," Amanda said, sounding more interested. "So this is going to be a major event."

"Oh, yeah," Kristin said. "And we need to line up dates soon."

"No problem," Amanda said. "I know who I'm going to invite."

"Who?" Kristin asked.

"Rick Hunter," Amanda said.

Elizabeth and I exchanged glances. What on earth was she talking about? Rick had already asked Mary to the dance.

"Rick Hunter?" Kristin asked. Apparently she was thinking the same thing we were. "But he's seeing Mary Wallace. I'm sure they're going together."

"Oh, really?" Amanda asked. "I didn't know that."

"Yeah, too bad, huh? Rick's so cute. You guys would look great together," Kristin said.

"Hmm. It is too bad," Amanda said.

"So who else do you want to ask?" Kristin wanted to know.

"That's just it. I can't think of anybody else," Amanda said.

Just then we saw Ms. Luster, the librarian, pass our table, and a second later we heard her say, "Girls! This library is for studying, not socializing!" She scolded Kristin and Amanda for another minute or so, which gave me and Elizabeth the chance to talk.

"Can you believe Amanda wanted to ask Rick out?" Elizabeth asked me. "I mean, it's so obvious he's dating Mary—how could she not know?"

I shrugged. "I guess she's not as smart as we thought."

"Well, if I were Mary, I wouldn't want Amanda going after my boyfriend," Elizabeth said.

"Rick would never go for her in a million years," I said. "Mary has nothing to worry about." Then I thought, *Why am I defending Mary? We're not even friends anymore.*

Old habits are hard to get rid of, I guess.

Play rehearsal went as awkwardly as usual on Monday, and on Tuesday I took the afternoon off. I went over to the day-care center before my lesson. It seemed like sticking to Tuesdays from now on was a good idea, since kids really like routine. Elizabeth was all ready to go with me when something came up with one of the sets at the last minute, and she had to stay for rehearsal after all.

On my bike ride over to the Center, I thought about how our big fight had taken place the Thursday before, and it had been five days since I'd talked to Lila, Ellen, Mary, or Mandy—if you didn't count angry notes. It wasn't getting any easier, but my grandmother told me that things like this took time, sometimes a lot of time. She also told me she thought we were crazy breaking up the Unicorns. The club had done so many good things around the community and had even helped her out, too. She didn't understand how things could have gotten so bad between us. I didn't really, either. It was like everything had changed overnight.

When I walked into the playroom, I almost fell over in shock. Mary was there. "What are you doing here?" I blurted, before I could stop myself.

She looked surprised—and a little hurt, too. "I can still come here, can't I?"

"Oh, uh, of course," I said. Then I hurried over to talk to Yuky, Arthur, and Oliver, who were making a huge poster with a ghost and a vampire on it.

"Hey, is that for the play we're doing?" I asked, sitting down in a small chair at the table where they were working.

Arthur nodded. "We told Mrs. Willard that we're going to the play, and she said we should make an ad for it, to put up at the front desk."

"That's a great idea!" I said.

"Can you help us with the letters?" Yuky asked.

I picked up a paintbrush. While I was working, in between breaking up fights between Arthur and Oliver over how much blood should be on the poster (it was about half covered with red paint so far), I heard Mary talking to Allison, Sandy, and Ellie. First she was reading them a fairy tale, and then she started talking about how she felt like *she* was in a fairy tale. Since Ellie's a little older, she wanted to hear all about the romance.

"Lila said there's a big dance coming up, and

she's going to wear a really beautiful dress," Ellie said. "And she said she's going with . . . What's his name?"

"Tommy," Mary said, laughing. "Yes, she does have a very pretty dress."

"Lila's so beautiful," Ellie said. "When I grow up I want to look just like her."

"So are you going to that dance, too?" Allison asked.

"Is it a ball, like the one Cinderella went to?" Sandy wanted to know.

"Well, not quite that fancy," Mary said. "It is only going to be in our school gym. But I bet the decorations will be really nice. And you know what? I've got a new dress, too, just like Lila."

"You do?" Ellie asked. "Who are you going with?"

"Rick, my boyfriend," Mary said.

"What's he like?"

"Very cute," Mary said. "The dress I bought was pretty expensive—a lot more than I'd usually spend. But I think it's going to be worth it. I think this dance is going to be the best one I've ever been to."

"Don't forget your shoe," Sandy said, then she, Allison, and Ellie started laughing.

As I added another letter to the giant poster, I couldn't help thinking that all this talk about the dance was for my benefit, not the kids'. Why did Mary feel that she had to brag about her new dress to me, though? OK, so maybe I didn't have a boyfriend, but that didn't mean I couldn't go to the dance, too. Just as Mandy and my grandmother had said.

When it was five o'clock, Mary picked up half the playroom, and I cleaned up the other half, wiping the table where we'd been painting and hanging the poster up to dry.

Mary stared at the poster for a second, just before she left. It seemed as if she was stalling, and I thought, *Maybe she wants to talk to me. Maybe the two of us could be friends again, even if we're not going to be Unicorns.* Mary and I were probably the most even-tempered of all our friends. If anyone could patch things up, we could.

"What is that?" she finally asked, pointing to a glob of white on the poster.

"A ghost," I said.

"Oh," she said. And then she walked out.

So much for patching things up.

Nine

On Wednesday, Elizabeth and I were walking down the hall to our lockers so we could drop off our books and Elizabeth could pick up her lunch. We planned to meet Jessica and Maria in a few minutes, so we were hurrying. I was telling her what had happened at the day-care center the afternoon before, how Mary was there and how we hadn't really spoken to each other—and how much I missed her.

Elizabeth shoved her books into her locker. She was getting out her lunch when I heard Rick and Tim behind us, at one of their lockers. I was going to say hello, but then I wondered if *they* wouldn't be talking to us, either, since they were the boy-friends of our ex-friends.

I couldn't believe what they were talking about.

I tugged Elizabeth's sleeve. "What?" she asked.

"Shh," I said, pointing behind me at Rick and Tim. They couldn't really see us because Elizabeth's locker door was open.

"I don't know what to do," Rick was saying. "I'm just not good at breaking up with girls."

"It's easy," Tim said. "Just tell her you're going to the dance with someone else."

Elizabeth's eyebrows shot up. "Did I just hear what I *think* I heard?" she whispered.

"I'm not going with someone else . . . yet," Rick said.

"Yeah, but you want to," Tim said. "Same difference."

Rick actually *wanted* to go to the semiformal with Amanda? That had to be who he was talking about. But I couldn't believe it. I mean, she was pretty, and she was an eighth grader, but how could he even think about breaking up with Mary, who was a hundred times nicer? Not to me lately, but still. She was a much better girlfriend to have than someone like Amanda.

I turned around and looked right at Rick. I wanted him to know that I'd heard what he was talking about. He looked at me nervously, then said, "Hi, Evie. Hi, Elizabeth."

"Hello," Elizabeth said slowly. "I didn't mean to eavesdrop, but did you just say you were thinking about going to the dance with someone besides Mary?"

"Uhh . . ." Rick seemed flustered.

I cleared my throat. It was time to bluff, if we wanted to find out whether what Rick was saying was what it sounded like. "You can tell us. You know, we're not even speaking to Mary anymore."

"Yeah, I heard," Rick said. "Well, I guess I can tell you, then. See, Amanda Harmon asked me to go with her. And not to be mean to Mary or anything, but I've always kind of liked Amanda."

"Kind of?" Tim scoffed.

"So you're going to take her instead of Mary?" I asked.

"But didn't you already make a date with Mary? I mean, isn't she kind of counting on it?" Elizabeth asked.

"Yeah, I did ask her, but that was a long time ago," Rick said. "And I've changed my mind."

I felt my heart start beating about twice as fast. What Rick was saying made me so angry! How could he drop Mary, just like that? And for Amanda! "So are you going to break up with her?" I asked. *Poor Mary*, I thought. *She's going to be so devastated.*

"I don't know," Rick said. "I mean, I really like Mary. But I think maybe what I'll do is just tell her at the last minute that I'm sick and I can't go. Then I'll go with Amanda."

Elizabeth's eyebrows shot up. "Really?"

"You mean, she'd just sit at home, and you'd be at the dance?" *Rick, you're acting like a total heel!* I wanted to say.

Rick nodded.

"Yeah, that's the best way to do it," Tim said. "That way she won't get upset and you won't have to deal with all that."

Won't get upset? When Mary found out the next day that Rick had shown up at the dance, not only feeling fine but with Amanda by his side, she wasn't going to be upset—she was going to be furious. *I* was furious, just imagining it. "So you're not planning on saying anything until then?" I asked. I thought about Mary's new dress, and how excited she'd been the day before.

"No, I guess not," Rick said. "I mean, I already told Amanda yes."

"So why not just break up with Mary now?" Elizabeth asked.

Rick shrugged. "I suppose I could, but . . . I don't know."

"Man, you've got some serious girl problems," Tim said. "Hey, let's grab some lunch before it's too late."

"OK. See you guys," Rick said. He turned to leave, but then he stopped and looked back at us. "Um, you're not going to say anything to Mary, are you?"

"Oh, no," I said, shaking my head and trying to look as though I didn't care *what* he did.

"Of course not. She won't even say hello to us," Elizabeth added. "We won't be talking to her anytime soon."

"Good. See you!" Rick called, walking off down the hall.

Elizabeth watched Rick for a minute. "You know, I always thought Rick was a pretty nice guy. But not anymore!"

"No kidding," I said. "Do you think he'll really go through with it and dump Mary like that?" We started down the hall toward the cafeteria.

"I wish I could say no, but you know how Amanda can be. I mean, if she wants to go to the dance with him, she's pushy enough to make it happen." Elizabeth picked up a scrap piece of paper that someone had dropped, and put it into the trash can.

"Well, what should we do?" I asked. "I know Mary's not a Unicorn anymore, but I still feel like I should defend her."

"Let's not do anything until we find out for sure whether he's going to do it," Elizabeth said. "There's no point hurting Mary if we don't have to, and it sounds like he's still deciding. I can't even *believe* what he just said, so I'm going to give him the benefit of the doubt—for now. I think we should keep this to ourselves, too. Let's not tell Jessica and Maria yet. I don't want it to get all over school," Elizabeth said.

"Good idea," I said. Jessica can't keep much to herself—in fact, it was amazing how quickly everyone had found out about the Unicorns split-ting up. Maybe Rick was just thinking about breaking up with Mary but wasn't going to go through with it. They'd only been dating for two weeks—how could he dump her, just like that?

I hadn't told Elizabeth about Mary buying a new, expensive dress just for the dance. Maybe she would end up going with Rick and wearing it after all. But if she didn't, she was going to be one sad Cinderella.

"Evie? Is something wrong? Are you not feeling well today?" Mr. Santos stopped playing in the middle of our piano and violin duet and looked over at me. It was Wednesday afternoon, and I was halfway through my lesson.

"What makes you say that?" I took my violin out from under my chin.

"I don't mean to criticize, but you're just not playing very well today," he said.

"I'm not?" I couldn't tell any difference between the way I had been playing and the way I usually played. Besides, this was a piece we'd practiced a dozen times already. "Haven't I been getting the notes right?"

"Oh, yes. Your playing is technically correct." Mr. Santos nodded. "But there is no emotion there. You seem to be just going through the motions, instead of feeling the music."

"I guess I have something on my mind," I admitted. "Something pretty big."

"Would it help to talk about it?" Mr. Santos asked. "You know, I have a good ear for things besides music."

I smiled. Even though Mr. Santos has only been my teacher for the past few months, we already do have a pretty close friendship. I felt as if I could confide in him. "OK. What if you knew something that someone else should know, too, only you weren't talking to that person anymore?"

Mr. Santos rearranged the sheet music on top of the piano. "Is this something very important?"

"Well, it might be," I said. "I'm not sure yet. The thing is, I was close friends with this person, but we had a major falling-out last week. And now I'm worried about her. I think maybe she's going to get hurt. But *she* was the one who didn't want to have anything to do with *me*—so why should I care about helping her?"

"That's easy," Mr. Santos said. "You're a good person, Evie. Just because you stopped being best friends, doesn't mean you don't still care about what happens to her, right?"

I nodded.

"Then you have your solution," Mr. Santos said.

"I should tell her?"

"I think you might feel better if you did."

I know the answer seemed really clear to him, and when I talked to him about it, it seemed obvious to me, too. But I'd felt so shut out by Mary when she stopped calling me. I didn't know if she deserved to know what I suspected about Rick. She was the one who thought spending time with him was so great that she didn't want to see us anymore. Maybe she should find out the truth on her own. I guess that sounds pretty harsh, but that's how I felt.

Maybe Elizabeth was right, I decided. If we waited, this whole thing would probably sort itself out, and we wouldn't have to get involved. There was no way Rick was going to go through with that lame plan he'd told us. If he really wanted to break up with her, he'd do it before publicly humiliating her at the dance. I was sure of it. At least that's what I told myself.

It was Wednesday, a week before the play's big opening night. Everything backstage was pretty well ready, though the kids doing the lights were having a hard time figuring out which lights to use when, and during rehearsal they kept flashing different colors all over the place.

"That's starting to drive me crazy," Elizabeth commented to me. "I think I'm getting a headache."

Jessica was trying on the letter sweater she'd wear during all of her scenes. "I wish I had more interesting clothes to wear," she said.

I saw Mandy look over at Jessica and roll her eyes. I knew that in Mandy's opinion, all the clothes decisions she had made were perfect. Actually, I agreed with her. I had to—I'd made half the decisions myself. I missed working with Mandy. And my grandmother missed seeing her, too. She'd told me so at breakfast that morning.

"Can't you figure out a way to work this out?" she had kept asking me. "No!" I'd kept saying.

. "Hey, Mary!" Mandy said in an excited voice. "What's up?"

Mary walked over to her and slumped into a chair. "I just made an appointment to get my hair trimmed. I want to make sure it looks good for the dance, so I'm getting it cut a couple of days before."

Jessica looked at me and raised one eyebrow. "Give me a break," she mouthed.

"Do you still want to get those makeovers at the mall this weekend?" Mandy asked.

"Definitely," Mary said. "Hey, did I tell you I talked to my mom last night about getting new shoes to go with my dress?"

"What did she say?"

"I couldn't believe it, but she actually said yes," Mary said. "She really likes Rick and she's happy for me. Of course, I have to kick in part of next month's allowance for them, but that's OK."

"You're going to look so fantastic!" Mandy cried. "We definitely have to take pictures that night."

I looked at Elizabeth. She looked as worried as I felt. Mary was getting ready for the dance of her life, and meanwhile Rick might be planning to tell her he wasn't even going to take her!

"Conference," Elizabeth said, gesturing toward the back door of the backstage area, which led out into a hallway.

"What for?" Jessica asked. "I need to be back soon for my next scene."

"It won't take long," Elizabeth said.

"I'll go get Maria," I said. I saw Mandy and Mary looking at us suspiciously, and I couldn't blame them. We were acting weird. But we had to talk about this now, before it got any worse.

Maria had just wrapped up a scene, so I asked her to come backstage with me. "What's going on?"

"It's a secret," I told her.

When we were all gathered in the hallway, and after we made sure no one else was within earshot, Elizabeth quickly explained what we'd overheard Amanda say, and then what Rick had told us.

"That's really weird," Maria said. "You know, someone in social studies today told me that Amanda was going to the dance with Rick. But I just thought she didn't know what she was talking about."

"Yeah, and I heard Amanda's friends talking about it at lunch," Jessica said. "But I figured it was just wishful thinking, because so many girls have crushes on Rick, especially now that he's starring in this play."

"I guess Rick decided," Elizabeth said to me. "And worse, it's already all over school, thanks to Amanda's big mouth. Mary's going to be so humiliated. Especially if he dumps her by just showing up at the dance with Amanda, while Mary sits at home, having the absolute worst night of her life."

"You should have heard her the other day, talking about the new dress she got," I said. "Now she's getting a makeover, and a haircut, and new pumps and—"

"Wait a second. If we've heard about it all over school, how come Mary hasn't heard anything about it yet?" Maria asked.

"I doubt anyone's going to tell *her*," Elizabeth said.

"That does it. We *have* to tell her," I said.

"Wait a second," Jessica said. "Why should we help her? She's the one who didn't want to be a Unicorn anymore. I think she should find out on her own. She didn't want us as friends—why should we be a good friend to her?"

"Jessica, how can you say that? Put yourself in her shoes," I said. "What if you were just hopelessly, helplessly in love with someone and he was about to dump you? And on top of that, make you look like a fool? Wouldn't you want to know?"

"Well, it'd never happen to me," Jessica said.

"Right," Maria said. "Sure it wouldn't. Come on, Jessica, it happens to everyone."

"What's even worse is that from the sound of things, the whole school's going to know about it when Rick shows up without her," Elizabeth said. "That's even more humiliating than Rick breaking up with her. *And* since everyone knows it's going to happen, they're going to think Mary's an idiot for not knowing."

"I agree we should tell her," Maria said. "I know we've had problems between us lately, but this is serious. The way I feel is, once a Unicorn, always a Unicorn, even if I haven't been one as long as you, Jessica."

"So let's tell her," I said. "This has been bugging me a lot over the past few days, and I just won't feel right unless we say something."

"OK, but once we tell her, then what?" Maria asked.

"What do you mean?" Elizabeth replied.

"We're going to help her get him back or something, aren't we?" Maria asked. "I mean, she's not just going to take this kind of thing from Rick. We have to stand up for her."

"What are you getting at?" Jessica asked. She sounded distrustful.

"I don't know if we can do this or not," Maria said. "It means everyone has to swallow a lot of pride. But if we really want to help Mary, we have to work together as a group. And maybe that means asking all the Unicorns to help."

"All the ex-Unicorns, you mean," Jessica said.

Maria nodded. "You have to admit, we did work great as a group. We managed to save the kids at the center during that big storm, we proved to everyone at school that we're the best club by getting back at the Eights . . ."

"Maria's right," Elizabeth said. "We can do more as a group than we can on our own. And the more members of the group who support Mary, the better she'll feel about this whole thing."

"So you're saying you want the whole club to meet?" I asked.

Maria and Elizabeth nodded. Jessica scuffed the toe of her sneaker against the concrete wall. "What do you say, Jessica?" Elizabeth asked.

She bit her lip. "I hate to think of anyone acting like a jerk to Mary. Even if she made some mistakes with us, she doesn't deserve that. And especially not when Amanda's involved!"

"Good. It's settled, then. We'll have a Unicorns reunion tomorrow afternoon," Elizabeth said. "We can have it at our house."

"Easier said than done," I commented.

"They wouldn't come last time—what makes you think they will this time?" Jessica asked.

"We're just going to have to convince them," Maria said. "Don't worry. I can be very persuasive when it comes to something as important as this."

Ten

"Maybe we should meet somewhere public," Mandy said. "You know, neutral territory." Elizabeth and I had approached Mandy and Lila by their lockers, right after school. So far they didn't seem very interested in getting together with us, and I can't say I blamed them.

"This isn't a duel," Elizabeth said. "And besides, this is something really private. I don't think we should have this conversation at Casey's. It's too serious," she said.

"I can't imagine what could be *that* serious," Lila said. "Are you going to yell at us about not spending time with you again?"

"No!" I said, a little more loudly than I'd meant to. "It's not about that at all. It has to do with . . . a friend."

"Which one?" Lila asked.

"We can't tell you now," I said.

"Come on, you guys. This is the last time I'll ever plead with you to do something, honest," Elizabeth said. "Just make sure you're there. It's really, really important, and you won't be sorry."

Lila looked at Mandy, who shrugged. "OK," Mandy said. "We'll be there. Lila, can you pick me up just before two?"

"Sure," Lila said. She turned to Elizabeth. "Nobody's sick or anything, are they?" There was genuine concern in her voice, so I knew she hadn't stopped caring about us, either. "Are someone's parents getting a divorce?"

"It's nothing like that," Elizabeth said, "but it is serious."

"OK. See you tomorrow," Lila said.

Jessica and Maria talked to Ellen and convinced her to come. I called Mary that night. Everyone thought that out of all the ex-Unicorns, I had the best chance of talking Mary into coming to the meeting.

"Hi, Mary, it's Evie," I said. "Please don't hang up, OK?"

"I won't," Mary said. "Evie, are you OK? You sound worried."

"Well, I'm just a little nervous, because I haven't talked to you in a week," I said. I took a deep breath. "But I have something to ask you."

"Go ahead," Mary said.

"I need you to come over to Jessica's house to-morrow," I said. "We're having a meeting."

"But I thought we weren't in a club anymore," she said.

"We're not. But there's something important we have to talk about, and you need to be there," I said. "I can't tell you anything else right now. But everyone else already agreed to come, even Lila, Mandy, and Ellen."

"They did?" Mary asked. She didn't say any-thing for a minute. "How come this is such a big secret?"

"It's something we have to talk about in per-son," I told her.

"Oh. Well, I'm supposed to meet Rick at four," Mary said.

I squirmed in my chair. Mary sure wouldn't want to meet him after what we had to tell her. But I couldn't say anything about that now. "The meet-ing's at two, so you'll have plenty of time," I said. "What do you say? Can you make it—please?"

"Sure," Mary said. "I'll see you tomorrow."

I couldn't sleep at all that night. I tried every-thing. I drank some warm milk, I listened to some quiet chamber music, I counted sheep (does that *ever* work?) . . . nothing. I just kept imagining the look on Mary's face when we told her about Rick, and how Amanda had convinced him to go to the dance with her instead of Mary. She was going to be *crushed*. And nothing we could do or say was going to make her feel any better.

I just hoped she'd let us help her get over him by being friends again. But I knew that was a lot to ask. No one we'd approached about the meeting seemed thrilled about the idea of the Unicorns getting together again.

"So." Mandy drummed her fingers against the arm of the couch. "Why are we here?"

"Does anyone want some more chips?" I passed the bag around for the tenth time that afternoon. "Here's the dip, too." I smiled at Mary as I handed the bowl to her. I couldn't help it. I was stalling because I was afraid of what was going to happen. Nobody was talking. Now that everyone was there, the eight of us were just sitting around, staring at the floor, the TV, the flowers on the coffee table. At anything but one another. You've heard the expression about the tension being so thick, you could cut it with a knife? You would have needed a *chain saw*. But at least everyone had shown up. I was grateful for that.

Elizabeth cleared her throat. "I guess we could get started." She gave me a nervous glance.

"Do you want me to start?" I asked.

Elizabeth nodded. "Tell them everything."

"I feel like we're here to find out who committed a murder," Lila said. "Why do you guys all look so serious?"

"You'll find out," Jessica told her. "Just hold on."

I looked at Mary, who was sitting in the rocking chair by the window. *Here goes everything,* I thought. "Mary, we found out something that we think we should tell you. And we wanted everyone to be here, because it's in times like these that the Unicorns have to stick together. Even if we haven't been a club lately, we have to be one now."

Mary seemed confused. "What does it have to do with me?"

I chewed my fingernail for a second. "It's about Rick," I said.

"What about him?" Lila asked.

"We found out a couple of things, totally by accident," I said. "OK, one day we heard Amanda telling Kristin she wanted to ask him to the dance. No big deal, right? Of course, we knew he was already going with you."

"Amanda likes Rick?" Mary said. "I didn't know that."

"Like he'd even look at her twice," Mandy said.

"That's what we thought," I said. "But then we heard Rick telling Tim something. He said he wasn't very good at breaking up with girls." I watched Mary's expression carefully. What I was saying seemed to be slowly filtering through. "We pretended we weren't friends with you anymore, so we could find out what he was talking about. He said he was thinking about pretending he was sick the night of the dance, so you wouldn't go, and *he* could show up with Amanda."

"What? That creep wants to go to the dance with Amanda, instead of Mary?" Lila cried. "Is that what you're saying?"

I nodded slowly. "We heard rumors about it at school, too."

"Rick's planning to break up with you, so he can go to the dance with Amanda," Elizabeth told Mary. "And everyone at school knows about it, which is the worst part. Amanda's been bragging to people about how she got him to split up with you."

Mary didn't say anything at first, but her face was turning pink. Then a tear slid down her cheek, then another, and another, until she was really crying. "I can't believe this," she said, wiping her face with her sleeve. Her voice was so sad and shaky, like a whisper. "How . . . how . . ." she sputtered, and then she burst out crying all over again.

Elizabeth handed her a tissue from the box on the coffee table. "I'm sorry," she said.

"Wait a second. If this is true, then how come we didn't hear about it?" Ellen asked.

"No one would tell you, because you're still Mary's best friends," Jessica said. "We only found out because Rick thought we weren't speaking to Mary anymore."

"Mary, I am so sorry," Mandy said. She went over and gave her a hug. "What a jerk!"

"No kidding," I said. "I can't believe anyone

would do something so low. You don't deserve to be treated like that, Mary. You're great!"

"Yeah, there's nothing wrong with you," Jessica said. "He's only doing it because Amanda pressured him into it, I bet."

"But . . . I bought that new dress. . . . I . . ." Mary muttered. "How can he be acting so nice to me when he's planning to stab me in the back? I don't get that. How could he have changed his mind about me, just like that?"

"He's a creep, that's how," Maria said.

"Boys don't know what they're doing," Jessica said. "No offense to anyone here. It's just sometimes they do incredibly dumb things."

"So wait a second. Do you know for sure that they're going together?" Mandy asked.

"Not one hundred percent for sure," I said. "But pretty close. That was Rick's plan a couple of days ago."

"Maybe we should find out for sure, then," Mandy said. "It's possible he changed his mind. I'm going to call Amanda."

"She'll never talk to you," Elizabeth said. "She hates us."

"Yeah, and I bet that's why she decided to go after Rick, too," Ellen said. "Because one of us was dating him, and she wanted to. She'd do anything to get under our skin."

"True, but . . . I bet she'd love to talk to us if she's really going to the dance with Rick," Mandy said.

"I bet she'll be bragging about it so much I'll have to hang up on her."

"Please do," Mary muttered through her tears.

Mandy went into the kitchen with Jessica. I could hear them talking, but I couldn't tell what they said.

"Mary, I'm sorry I had to give you such bad news," I said. "I know it must hurt a lot. I just didn't want you to get even more hurt later."

Mary nodded. "I know."

"And if there's anything I can do, anything at all, you'll tell me, right?" I said.

She nodded again. After her initial outburst, it seemed as though she was too choked up to say anything else.

Mandy and Jessica came back into the living room a minute later. They weren't smiling. "Sorry, Mary. It looks like Evie's right," Mandy said.

"Amanda told us she's going to the dance with him," Jessica said. "We even called Peter, to make sure."

"He didn't want to rat on his friend, but he told me she's right," Mandy said. "Rick's planning to tell you he's sick with the flu, and then go to the dance with Amanda. Like you wouldn't find out." Mandy shook her head.

Mary slumped down even lower in the rocking chair. "He must think I'm so stupid."

"So what should we do?" I asked. "Elizabeth and I wanted to have this meeting so we could all think of what to do together."

"What's there to do?" Mary asked. "He's dumping me, and that's that. I just won't meet him later, and when he asks me why, I'll tell him I found out the truth. That he's a complete jerk."

"No, that's not good enough. We have to do something to get back at him," Jessica told her. "Mary, if we hadn't found out about this, he was going to make you look like a fool."

"Well, I know what I would do. *I'd* like to strangle him," Ellen said.

"And I'd like to put dishwashing soap in his soda, Monday at lunch," Maria said.

"And I hope he has an absolutely rotten time at the dance," Mary said. "I hope his pants rip."

"Hold on, you guys. We're after *real* revenge here," Jessica said. "Between the eight of us, there has to be something really terrible we could do to embarrass him in front of everyone."

Nobody said anything for a couple of minutes. I kept trying to think of some way to humiliate Rick the way he'd planned to humiliate Mary. Could she dump him, maybe? But that wouldn't be very hard on him if he already planned on breaking up with her.

I looked around the room. All the Unicorns seemed as though they were concentrating really hard, using all their brainpower. When we all get behind something, it's amazing what we can come up with, even if at that moment I didn't have an idea in my head.

"It's obvious, isn't it? There's only one thing to

do," Lila said excitedly after a few more minutes. "I can't believe I didn't think of it right away!"

"It better be good. Because there's no way we're going to let some guy trample all over a Unicorn's heart," Ellen said.

"Right," Lila said. "And here's how we can do it. Rick just happens to have a starring role in the play. We can take advantage of that, big time."

"What do you mean?" Elizabeth asked.

"He's already going to be up onstage, in front of the entire school, everyone's parents, their friends, all the teachers," Lila said. "If we really want to get revenge, that's where we should do it."

"How?" Maria asked.

"I get it!" Jessica said excitedly. "We can do something to make Rick look really bad up there. Something like . . . OK, Mary, you said maybe his pants could rip at the dance. Mandy, couldn't you guys rig some of his clothes so they fall off in the middle of a scene?"

"I don't know if we want all his clothes to fall off," I said. "That's kind of too much."

"OK, but he could rip his pants," Jessica said.

"Right," Maria said. "And we could also make him look stupid if he started messing up his lines."

"How could we do that?" Mary asked. "He has them all memorized already."

"Most actors learn their lines around what the other actors' lines are," Maria explained. "If we said ours wrong, he'd get thrown off."

"We could also write a new scene, or part of one, where we tell him what a jerk he is," Lila said. "And as stage manager, I'll be very happy to set up everything for that."

"I don't know, you guys," Mary said. "That sounds pretty intense. Are you sure we couldn't just talk to him or something?"

"NO!" we all screamed at once.

"Mary, he was going to humiliate you in front of the whole school. We should show him what that feels like," Mandy argued.

"Won't it wreck the play?" I asked. "I'd hate for it to be bad, after everyone's hard work."

"Yeah, won't Mr. Drew kill us?" Elizabeth asked.

Ellen shook her head. "You guys are so chicken. All we have to do is change part of one scene. When Mr. Drew asks us about it, I'll just tell him I forgot my lines and we improvised. He'll believe *that*." She smiled. Even though Ellen can be an airhead, she's great about sticking up for her friends. And at least she knows she's spacey.

"OK. So what we need to do is write the new lines and start practicing them," Jessica said. "I'll get some paper."

While she was gone, I turned to Mary. "How are you doing?"

She smiled. "A lot better, now. Only, I don't know what I'm going to do with my new dress. My mom's going to be really upset that we bought it for nothing."

"Excuse me, but you don't have to have a date to go to the dance," Jessica interrupted. "I'm going, and I don't have one."

"Me, too," I said.

"I thought you weren't—" Mandy began to protest.

"I changed my mind," I said, and smiled at her.

"Good," she said. "Now, did you pick out what dress you're going to wear from the Attic yet? Because I saw this great little black antique cocktail dress that I think would look really cool on you, with some gloves, maybe a hat . . ."

It felt fantastic to be hanging out as a group again. I just hoped we could make it last this time.

Eleven

The next week really flew by. We were all busy making our final preparations for the play. And, of course, practicing the new scene we'd added. Elizabeth and Maria had written it together, and Jessica and Ellen were rehearsing new lines. Mandy and I had changed one of Rick's outfits ever so slightly.

Meanwhile, Mary wasn't sure whether to be nice to Rick or not. Of course, she didn't *want* to be, but she didn't want to give anything away, either, so she pretty much just avoided him as much as she could. That wasn't easy, in our school. And Amanda? Well, we made sure we sent as many evil looks her way as humanly possible. (Since we don't normally get along with her, this wasn't such a big change.) Rick was still holding off on officially breaking his date with Mary, but there was a lot of gossip around school about how Amanda wanted him to do it. I even heard some of the boys had a betting pool on which day he'd dump Mary. Talk about heartless.

Wednesday was opening night, and I already knew it was completely sold out. Still, it was a surprise when I got to school around six thirty and saw how many people were milling around in the halls. I peeked into the auditorium to see how many seats had been filled. Outside of school assemblies, I couldn't ever remember seeing *every* seat taken.

"Evie, I'm going to sit down now. Good luck back there." My grandmother kissed me on the cheek. "I'm really proud of you."

Don't say anything yet! I almost told her. If our little revenge scheme ruined the play, I'd feel terrible. But I was pretty sure we'd worked it out carefully enough that all the kids in school would know what was going on but the rest of the audience would be confused. Besides, it *was* only one scene. I hadn't even told my grandmother what we were planning, and I usually tell her everything. "Thanks, Grandma," I said. "And thanks for helping us with the clothes."

"My pleasure," she said. Then she spotted Mary's mother, and the two of them went into the auditorium together.

"Evie!" Yuky was running down the hall toward me, her black patent leather shoes clicking against the linoleum. Sandy and Allison, the Terrible

Twosome, were right behind her, with Mr. Meyer bringing up the rear.

"Hi! I'm so glad you came," I said, as Yuky wrapped her arms around my leg.

"Is this where you go to school?" Sandy asked.

I nodded.

Sandy looked around the hallway, at the trophy case and all the pictures and posters on the walls. "It's nice."

"Well, you'll be here pretty soon," I told her. "Right?"

"No way," Sandy said, seriously.

"Thank you so much for getting tickets for the girls, Evie," Mr. Meyer said. "This is a real treat."

"You're welcome," I said. "I hate to run off, but I need to get backstage and make sure everything's going OK. We'll see you guys after the play, OK? Come backstage for the party and you can have some cake."

"Yea! A party!" Yuky cried. "'Bye, Evie."

I went around outside to the back of the auditorium, to the door leading to the backstage area. When I went into the girls' dressing room, Jessica, Maria, Carmen, and Ellen were sitting in front of the mirrors, putting the finishing touches on their makeup with help from Mrs. Riteman. (She used to work in theater as a makeup artist, back in college.)

"Wow, you guys look amazing!" I said.

"Hi, Evie," Ellen said, and she smiled at me. "I am so nervous, I feel like I'm going to explode."

"Ellen, you're going to do fine," her mother said.
"Yeah, we've all seen you in rehearsal," I said.
"And this week you had everything down cold."

"Besides, if you do start to forget, Jessica and I can help you out," Maria said.

It was going to be a much better play, now that all the Unicorns were actually speaking to one another again!

Mandy, Elizabeth, Lila, and I were standing in the wings, watching the whole play. So far it was going really well, but now was the time that really counted.

"Rick looks so innocent out there," Elizabeth whispered.

Lila grinned. "He has no idea what's about to happen."

Maria, Ellen, and Rick were nearing the end of the last scene of Act Two. In the regular scene, Rick (Victor) was supposed to tell Ellen (Mallory) all about his special powers and how he got them. He had just finished explaining when Maria burst in.

"Look, if you don't want to ask Mary—I mean, Mallory—to the homecoming dance, then you should just be honest and tell her that, instead of making up some story about being a vampire," Maria said. "Because I'd rather go with you, anyway, so just get rid of her."

"Huh?" Rick said. He was starting to look really uncomfortable.

"What about me? Don't I deserve to be told what's going on?" Ellen asked. "I thought we were going to the dance."

"What dance? What are you talking about?" Rick asked.

"Like you don't know," Maria said. "You can't go with two girls, can you? So you have to pick which one you really want."

"But—" Rick looked out at the audience, as if asking them to help him out of the scene.

Ellen grabbed one side of Rick, and Maria grabbed the other. One of them was holding on to his belt. Everyone in the audience was laughing hysterically as they pulled him one way, then the other.

Jessica bounded onto the stage, ready for her Freshman role. "You know, cheaters never prosper," she said. "The easiest way isn't always the right way. Honesty is the best policy."

"And creeps are the lowest life-form on earth!" Ellen added. She tugged Rick one last time, and his belt came flying off, sliding across the stage. Ellen staggered backward, almost losing her balance.

Rick's pants dropped from his waist to his hips, and they were about to go down even farther when Rick grabbed the waistband to hold them up.

Now everyone in the audience was howling.

"You can have him. I don't want to go to the dance with him!" Ellen declared.

"Neither do I!" Maria said.

"Victor, if you get lonely, here's a quarter." Jessica tossed a coin at him. "Call someone who cares."

Then all three girls ran off the stage, leaving Rick standing there all by himself. He obviously had no clue about what to do next. The audience clapped and cheered.

There were a few moments of complete silence after the laughter from the audience died down. They waited for Rick to continue. He glanced toward the wings, where Mandy and I were watching, then to the other side, where Mr. Drew was standing.

"What do I do now?" Rick asked him in a loud stage whisper. The audience cracked up all over again, and Mr. Drew pulled the curtain.

"You guys were so unbelievably funny," I told Ellen at the backstage party after the play. "I laughed so hard, my stomach *still* hurts."

"Do you think we got him back?" Jessica asked.

"Oh, yeah," Mandy said, nodding. "And then some."

"When his pants almost fell down, I thought I was going to lose it," Maria said. "That's why we ran offstage so fast."

"Jessica!" a familiar voice screamed. I turned around and saw Oliver running full-tilt toward us. "Jessica, you're a star!" he cried.

"Hey there," she said, bending down to give

him a hug. "Thanks. Did you like it?"

"Well, it was kind of boring for a while, but then it got better," Oliver said.

Ellie came over, too, with her mother, Mr. Stillman, and Mr. Fowler. "I liked it when you were trying to pull the vampire in half," she said. "And his pants almost came off!" She giggled.

Elizabeth poked me in the ribs. "Look out, everybody, here comes Mr. Drew."

"Uh-oh," I said. Mr. Drew was heading straight for us, and he didn't look too thrilled, even though everyone else backstage seemed to think the play had been a major success.

"Excuse me. Ellen, Jessica, may I speak to you for a moment?" Mr. Drew asked. "Mandy and Evie, you, too." He stepped to the side, and we all walked over toward him. I heard the rest of the Unicorns taking a few steps, too, so they'd be within earshot. I hoped Mr. Drew wasn't too angry. We still had three more performances to do, and I didn't want him to kick us off those. Not that he could get anyone else to take over on such short notice. It wasn't as if Ellen had an understudy or anything.

"Now, can you girls tell me what happened at the end of the second act?" Mr. Drew asked.

Jessica gave him her best "I'm so innocent it hurts" look, the one she uses on teachers and Mr. Clark all the time. I swear, she's been practicing it her entire life. "What are you talking about?" she asked.

Mr. Drew cleared his throat. "I hardly think I should have to explain. First there were some different lines being said out there, lines that were not in my original script."

"Oh," Ellen said with a little laugh. "I'm sorry, Mr. Drew. That was my fault. I lost track of where we were. You know me, I *always* had trouble with that scene in rehearsal."

"You did? Funny, I don't remember that." Mr. Drew scratched his head.

"Oh, yeah. We were always messing that up," Maria said. "I guess because there's so many of us in that scene. You know, it gets kind of confusing, even for me."

"Hmm. All right, but what about the fact that you all left the stage at the same time—and Rick was still standing there? That was not supposed to happen, and you all have to know that," Mr. Drew argued.

"I thought Rick messed up," Ellen said. "Wasn't he supposed to leave with us?"

"And leave an empty stage at the end of the act?" Mr. Drew looked horrified. "No, no, no! The scene ends, and the curtain closes, and *then* you leave."

"I guess we just got overexcited or something," Jessica said. "Mr. Drew, it *is* opening night."

"Meaning?" Mr. Drew asked.

"We were all really nervous," Jessica said. "Don't worry, we'll get it right tomorrow night."

"Yeah, it was a major case of the jitters, that's all," Ellen said. "I'm sorry. I'll be better tomorrow."

"Well . . ." Mr. Drew seemed convinced. "All right. And by the way, except for that scene, you all did a terrific job. I'm pleased with the performance." He smiled. "Now, go have some cake."

I looked at Ellen and let out a huge sigh of relief. She nodded, and we all started to walk toward the refreshment table. Then I felt a tap on my shoulder. "Evie? Mandy? I still have a question for you," Mr. Drew said.

"Sure, Mr. Drew," Mandy said. "What's up?"

Mr. Drew frowned. "It's not what's up. It's what almost came down." He stared down at me.

I looked right into his eyes. "What do you mean?" My voice came out almost in a whisper, because I was holding my breath.

"Rick's trousers?" Mr. Drew said.

Mandy laughed, and he glared at her. "I'm sorry—I know it's not funny," she said, taking on a more serious look. "Mr. Drew, I really don't know what happened there. I guess that belt was a little too old. We did have to scrimp on the wardrobe, you know."

"Even so. Would you take care to see that things will . . . hold up, shall we say, tomorrow night?" Mr. Drew asked.

"Oh, definitely," I said. "I promise we'll double-check everything."

"I'm just wondering. Why were those trousers

so big on him in the first place?" Mr. Drew asked.

"It's how everyone's wearing them in New York," Mandy said. "We're just trying to make sure he stays in character."

"Uh-huh. Well, at least the rest of the clothes held out fine. Thanks for doing a good job," Mr. Drew said.

Mandy and I only got a few feet away before we cracked up laughing.

Twelve

All during the backstage party, Rick had kind of been standing in the corner with some of his friends. The rest of the couples were together. Tommy was hanging out with Lila, Tim had brought Ellen a rose (some people really do change, I guess), and Mandy and Peter were entertaining some of the little kids and laughing.

When one of Rick's friends walked over to the refreshment table, Jessica said, "OK, here's our chance. Let's go."

"Go where?" Mary asked.

"To tell him off!" Jessica said. "What else?"

Mary shook her head. "You can if you want, but I'm not going over there."

"Well, at least come and listen," Jessica said. "You can stand behind that piece of the set over there."

Mary tugged my sleeve, and I went with her. "Kind of nice to have someone like Jessica around when things get bad, isn't it?" I asked her. "She's like a watchdog."

She nodded. "It's kind of nice to have everyone around, actually."

"Rick, can I talk to you for a second?" Jessica said politely.

I peeked around the corner of the backdrop. Rick was glaring at her. "What about? Didn't you say everything already? You know, you could have just *told* me everyone knew what was going on."

"And *you* could have just acted like a decent person and told Mary first, instead of your buddies," Jessica said.

"Well, you still didn't have to humiliate me on-stage in front of the whole school," Rick complained.

Jessica shrugged. "That's what happens when you try to mess with the Unicorn Club. We stick up for our friends. And Mary's the best friend anyone could ever have. It's too bad you were too dumb to figure that out." Then, without another word, Jessica walked off.

"You know what, Evie? You're going to kill me, but I feel kind of bad for him," Mary said.

"Mary! After what he did to you?" I asked.

"I know I shouldn't," Mary said. "But we did have a lot of fun together before he started acting like a jerk." She sounded as if she was about to start crying.

I put my arm around her shoulder. "I know," I said. I tried to think of something to make her feel better. "But someday you'll have fun with someone who doesn't act like a creep, too," I said.

Mary smiled at me. "You sound like that dumb advice column in *Teen Talk*."

"OK, maybe I have read a few too many issues lately," I said, laughing. "Maybe I should cancel my subscription."

When I was leaving with my grandmother a few minutes later, Mandy came over to me. "Casey's tomorrow afternoon at two. Be there," she said, then she went over to Elizabeth to tell her the same thing.

Casey's looked as though it were having a theme party on Saturday afternoon. There were two tables pushed together, and everyone had so much purple on, it was almost funny. Jessica even ordered black raspberry ice cream, because it was lavender-colored. Besides that, about half of us had worn our Unicorn jackets.

"Did you hear what happened? Amanda told Rick there was no way she wanted to go to the dance with him after last night's disaster," Lila said triumphantly. She ate a spoonful of pecan praline ice cream. I'd gotten rocky road, my favorite.

"Good," Jessica said. "I hope he has a rotten time."

"Speaking of the dance, we should look for

some clothes after we eat," I said. "I still haven't found anything to wear."

"What about that dress I told you about, the little black one?" Mandy asked. "It'll look adorable on you."

"I went to the store this morning with my grandmother. It was sold already," I told her.

"Rats," Mandy said. "Well, yeah. I could go for a little shopping. What about you guys?"

"Sure," Lila said.

"Don't you have to meet Tommy or something?" Jessica asked, raising her eyebrows accusingly.

Lila frowned. "No."

"You guys didn't break up, did you?" Maria asked.

"Of course not," Lila said. "We just don't happen to have plans today."

"Not to ruin a party or anything, but maybe we should talk about that," Elizabeth said.

"About what?" Mandy asked.

"Well, we still haven't talked about the reason we fought and split up in the first place," Elizabeth said. She twirled an extra spoon around on the table. "I mean, it's great that we pulled together last week, but . . . well, what's going to happen next week? Are you guys going to spend all your time with your boyfriends again?"

I had to admire Elizabeth's courage. I wanted to talk about that stuff, too, but I was kind of figuring maybe it'd just work itself out. Then again, maybe not, and we'd all be fighting again in a week.

"We all made it here today, didn't we?" Ellen snapped.

Jessica nodded. "Yeah. But what about the next time?"

"The thing is, we won't always be dating boys, but sometimes we might be," Elizabeth said. She was tearing off little pieces of her napkin. "And we have to figure out a way to deal with that."

"Well, maybe we should make up some new rules," Mandy said. She took a sip of her strawberry shake.

"Great, just what we need," Lila muttered under her breath. But of course, everyone heard her.

"OK, Miss President," I said, trying to keep the mood light. "What did you have in mind?"

"Rule number one," Jessica blurted out before Mandy could answer me. "When we need to have a meeting, everyone has to come, no matter what. Unless someone has the flu, in which case, stay home, because I don't want to catch it."

"And secondly, we should have meetings once a week, at least," Mandy said.

"Give me a break," said Ellen. "I'll probably never see Tim again."

"Hey, let's not fight," said Mandy. "How about every other week?"

"All right. I can live with that," Ellen said.

"Rule three. We're not allowed to ignore our friends for our boyfriends like we did before,"

Mandy said. "I guess I didn't realize how much we were doing that, because I was so excited about being with Peter. But I know if it had been the other way around, I would have been mad, too."

"And we know that if we were in your shoes, we might have done the same thing," I said.

"No way!" said Jessica. "I never would have treated my best friends that way."

I looked at Jessica, then at the others. Were we really all friends again? "Come on, Jessica, seriously. I can see how they'd want to hang out with their boyfriends all the time. It doesn't mean it's right, but I can understand it."

"I guess we *were* pretty rude," Lila said, looking pointedly at Jessica.

"Wait a second. Somebody get a tape recorder," Elizabeth joked.

"Lila's admitting she was rude?" Jessica rubbed her ear. "I must be hearing things."

Lila tossed the cherry off the top of her sundae at Jessica, and it bounced off her shoulder. "Look, can't I even apologize?" she asked.

"You may," Maria said.

"I guess I was being pretty selfish," Lila said. "All you guys wanted was for us to come to one meeting, but I just couldn't break my plans with Tommy."

"Would you now?" Elizabeth asked.

"Yeah," Lila said. "As long as we don't have meetings on Friday nights anymore."

"Mary, how do you feel about all this?" Mandy asked. "You haven't said a word."

Mary shrugged. "It sounds fine. But I want to add another rule, OK?"

"Sure, what is it?" I asked.

"Rule number four. No one is allowed to date a jerk!" she said. "And if anyone does, then it's up to all of us to tell her to break up with him."

"*If* she'll listen," Jessica put in.

"Yeah," said Lila. "I know a few people at this table who are pretty stubborn."

Mandy laughed uneasily, then looked at Mary and smiled. "OK. It's a deal. Right, everybody?"

Everyone nodded, although I'm not sure if Jessica, Lila, and Ellen really agreed. It was funny how we'd all pulled together so well last night, and now we were already snapping at one another again. I wondered how long the peace among the Unicorns could last.

"I think that's enough rules for one day," Ellen said. "I won't be able to remember more than four, anyway."

"Is your memory all full of play lines?" Maria asked.

"Yeah, and what's going to be really hard is to do that scene *right* tonight. It was so much more fun the way we did it last night," Ellen said.

"Well, we can't do that again," Mandy said. "We owe Mr. Drew one flawless performance, at least."

"Then let's talk about something else," Jessica

said. "For instance, the semiformal. It's tomorrow night and I don't have a date—"

"You don't have a date?" Lila asked. "What have you been doing, hiding under a rock?"

"Hey! I don't have one, either," I said.

"Neither do I," Mary said.

She looked kind of sad, so no one said anything for a minute.

Then Jessica said, "There's only one thing to do. All of us should go, dates or not. Nothing says we have to have a date. Besides, there'll probably be some cute guys there. I mean Rick's going. . . ."

Everyone cracked up.

We all decided to go shopping after we finished our ice cream. It felt good to be doing something as a group again. All eight of us. But listening to everyone argue over how things were going to be done in the future, I wondered if the Unicorn Club even *had* a future.

Things are OK for now, but will the peace among the Unicorns last? Find out in THE UNICORN CLUB #6: **The Unicorns at War**.

SIGN UP FOR THE SWEET VALLEY HIGH® FAN CLUB!

Hey, girls! Get all the gossip on Sweet Valley High's® most popular teenagers when you join our fantastic Fan Club! As a member, you'll get all of this really cool stuff:

- Membership Card with your own personal Fan Club ID number
- A Sweet Valley High® Secret Treasure Box
- Sweet Valley High® Stationery
- Official Fan Club Pencil (for secret note writing!)
- Three Bookmarks
- A "Members Only" Door Hanger
- Two Skeins of J. & P. Coats® Embroidery Floss with flower barrette instruction leaflet
- Two editions of *The Oracle* newsletter
- Plus exclusive Sweet Valley High® product offers, special savings, contests, and much more!

Be the first to find out what Jessica & Elizabeth Wakefield are up to by joining the Sweet Valley High® Fan Club for the one-year membership fee of only $6.25 each for U.S. residents, $8.25 for Canadian residents (U.S. currency). Includes shipping & handling.

Send a check or money order (do not send cash) made payable to "Sweet Valley High® Fan Club" along with this form to:

SWEET VALLEY HIGH® FAN CLUB, BOX 3919-B, SCHAUMBURG, IL 60168-3919

NAME _____
(Please print clearly)

ADDRESS _____

CITY_____ STATE _____ ZIP_____
(Required)

AGE _____ BIRTHDAY_____ / _____ / _____

Your friends at Sweet Valley High have had their world turned upside down!

Meet one person with a power so evil, so dangerous, that it could destroy the entire world of Sweet Valley!

A Night to Remember, the book that starts it all, is followed by a six book series filled with romance, drama and suspense.